Andy Griffiths is one of Australia's funniest and most successful writers. His books have sold over 3 million copies worldwide, have featured on the *New York Times* bestseller lists, and have won over 30 Australian children's choice awards.

TREASURE FEVER!

ANDY GRIFFITHS

PAN
Pan Macmillan Australia

First published 2008 in Pan by Pan Macmillan Australia Pty Limited
1 Market Street, Sydney

Reprinted 2008 (twice), 2009, 2012 (twice)

National Library of Australia
Cataloguing-in-Publication data:

Griffiths, Andy, 1961–

Treasure fever! / author, Andy Griffiths.

Sydney : Pan Macmillan, 2008.

978 0 330 42389 2 (pbk.)

Schooling around ; no. 1
Griffiths, Andy, 1961– Schooling around

For children.

Humorous stories, Australian.
Children's stories, Australian.

A823.4

Illustration by Nathan Jurevicius
Typeset in 12/16 pt New Aster by Post Pre-press Group
Printed in Australia by McPherson's Printing Group

Papers used by Pan Macmillan Australia Pty Ltd are natural, recyclable products made from wood grown in sustainable forests. The manufacturing processes conform to the environmental regulations of the country of origin.

For Miss S

Once upon a time

Once upon a time there was—and still is—a school called Northwest Southeast Central School.

Northwest Southeast Central School is located in the southeast of a town called Northwest, which is located to the northwest of a big city called Central City.

You don't need to know where Central City is, because it's not important. What *is* important is the school. In this school there is a classroom. And in that classroom there is a fifth-grade class. Most important of all, in that class of fifth-grade students there is a student named Henry McThrottle who likes telling stories.

That's where I come in.

I'm Henry McThrottle . . . and this is my latest story.

A very unusual morning

It all started one morning when our teacher, Mrs Chalkboard, was late for class.

Now you might not think that's so remarkable, but believe me, it was for Mrs Chalkboard. Because Mrs Chalkboard was *never* late. She was usually there on the dot at 8.36 am, but that particular morning 8.36 am came and went and there was still no Mrs Chalkboard.

Not that anybody seemed to mind very much.

Clive Durkin was amusing himself by chewing up little bits of paper and flicking them at people.

Jack Japes was bent over his desk drawing cartoons. Jack was always drawing cartoons. He's the best drawer in the class.

Gretel Armstrong, the strongest girl in the school, was arm wrestling with herself. She had to do this because nobody else would arm wrestle with her. Jenny Friendly was cheering her on. It seemed like Gretel's left arm was winning.

Grant Gadget was madly pushing buttons on some sort of electronic device. Grant Gadget was *always* pushing buttons on some sort of electronic device.

Gina and Penny Palomino were grooming the long rainbow-coloured manes of their toy horses. Gina and Penny were *always* grooming their toy horses. And if they weren't doing that they were riding imaginary horses around the school. Gina and Penny *loved* horses.

The rest of the class was engaged in activities of more or less importance. Mostly less.

The only people who seemed at all worried by Mrs Chalkboard's non-arrival were the class captains, Fiona McBrain and David Worthy. David kept looking anxiously at his watch and checking it against the clock on the wall. Fiona was standing at the door of the classroom and peering down the corridor. 'Still not here!' she said. 'I can't believe Mrs Chalkboard is *still* not here!'

Suddenly, Jenny grabbed my arm. 'Henry!' she said. 'Something's wrong with Newton!'

I looked across at Newton Hooton. He was clutching his desk as if it was going to float away if he didn't hold it to the ground. His face was white. His eyes were shut tight. I could see that he was on the verge of a panic attack.

Now the thing you've got to understand about Newton Hooton is that this wasn't particularly unusual. Newton was pretty much *always* on the verge of a panic attack.

Newton, you see, was scared of, well, everything! Spiders, busy roads, heights, lightning, cotton buds, butterflies . . . you name it, he was scared of it. I wasn't sure what had made him so scared this time. All I knew was that he was more scared than I'd ever seen him.

Jenny and I got up and went over to him.

'Newton!' I said, putting my hand on his shoulder. 'What's the matter?'

Newton gulped. He blinked and stared at me with big round eyes as if he'd never seen me before.

'M-Mrs Chalkboard!' said Newton. 'Sh-she's late!'

'It's okay!' said Jenny, putting her hand on Newton's other shoulder and patting it lightly. 'She's just a little bit late, that's all.'

'B-b-but she's never late!' stammered Newton. 'Wh-what if she doesn't come? What then?'

'Then they'll send a substitute,' said Jenny. 'Everything will be fine. Her car has probably just broken down.'

'She's probably just been held up in traffic,' I offered.

'Impossible,' said Fiona, returning from her vigil at the door. 'Mrs Chalkboard doesn't have a car. She catches the bus.'

'Ah, yes,' I said. 'Good point. Thanks for your help, Fiona.'

'Don't mention it,' said Fiona, completely missing my sarcasm.

'What if she's been in an accident?' said Newton.

'I don't think that's likely,' said Jenny. 'You know how careful Mrs Chalkboard is.'

'Yes, but careful people can still be involved in accidents,' said Fiona. 'That's why they are called *accidents*. Something may have happened to the bus.'

Newton's face was getting whiter and whiter, if that was even possible.

'Yeah,' said Jack, taking up where Fiona left off. 'There might have been an oil spill on the road and the bus skidded and went over a cliff . . . into shark-infested water . . . and the sharks got into the bus and all the passengers got eaten alive . . . and all that was left was their skeletons. Then imagine if Mrs Chalkboard's skeleton climbed back up the cliff and hitched a ride to school and then came in the classroom and—'

'JACK!' said Jenny, 'for goodness' sake, STOP IT! You're scaring Newton to death! I'm sure Mrs Chalkboard is fine!'

'Then where is she?' said Fiona, getting up and checking the corridor again. 'She should be here by now. We're supposed to be doing maths.'

'So what's the problem?' said Clive. 'We're supposed to be doing maths and we're *not* doing maths! That's *good*, isn't it?'

'But I *like* maths!' said Fiona.

'Me too!' said David.

'I hate maths!' said Clive. 'You two should get your brains examined.'

'You should *get* a brain, Clive,' said David. 'Maybe you'd enjoy maths more.'

'You'd better watch your mouth, Worthy,' said Clive, 'or else.'

'Or else what?' said David.

'Or else,' said Clive, 'I'll tell my brother what you said. And I can tell you now, he's not going to like it.'

'Tell your brother whatever you want,' said David. 'He doesn't scare me.'

'I'm going to tell him that you said that, too,' said Clive. 'You're going to be sorry. You're going to be *really* sorry! You're going to be *really, really*—'

Newton's eyes were almost popping out of his head.

'Everyone,' pleaded Jenny, 'could you please PLEASE PLEASE stop talking about scary things. You're upsetting Newton!'

6

'He's a cry-baby,' said Clive.

'And you've got a big mouth!' I said.

'I'm going to tell my brother you said that,' said Clive. 'And I can tell you now, he's not going to like it.'

'Is there a single thing in the world your brother *does* like?' I asked.

'Yeah,' said Clive. 'Beating people up. He *really* likes that. My brother's really tough. He could beat up this whole class, all at the same time, if he wanted.'

Newton yelped. The thought of Clive's brother, Fred Durkin, beating up the whole class was clearly too much for him.

Poor Newton.

If he'd only known what *he* was going to end up doing to Fred Durkin!

But, then, it's probably just as well that he didn't know. That *definitely* would have been too much for him.

3
Principal Greenbeard

Suddenly Fiona ran from the door back to her desk. 'Shush, everyone,' she said. 'Here comes Principal Greenbeard . . . and he's got somebody with him!'

Something was obviously up. Maybe Mrs Chalkboard really *had* had an accident.

At the mention of Principal Greenbeard's name, Newton gasped.

'It's going to be okay, Newton,' I said.

Newton just stared at me, too scared to speak.

Jenny and I each gave him one last pat and then went back to our seats.

We had just sat down when Principal Greenbeard and another man walked into the room.

Principal Greenbeard, dressed in a white naval uniform like the captain of a ship, saluted the class.

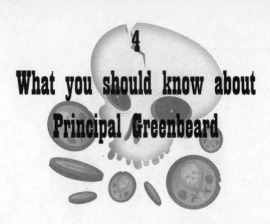

4
What you should know about
Principal Greenbeard

Now, before I go on, what you should know about Principal Greenbeard is that he's not actually the captain of a ship. He just loves ships and sailing.

And when I say he loves ships and sailing, I mean he *really* loves ships and sailing.

In fact, he loves ships and sailing so much that he acts as if the school is one huge ship, that all the teachers and students are sailors, and that he, of course, is the captain.

It's important that you know this, otherwise you might think he is a bit crazy.

Well, obviously he is a *bit* crazy, but he isn't *all* crazy. He's just crazy about anything to do with ships and sailing.

5
Mr Brainfright

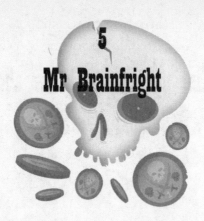

'Good morning, crew,' said Principal Greenbeard.

We all jumped to our feet and saluted him. We were well trained.

'Good morning, Principal Greenbeard,' we all chanted. Well, all except for Newton, who just sat there, frozen.

'I'd like you to welcome a new member of the crew aboard the good ship *Northwest Southeast Central*,' he said. 'This is Mr Brainfright. He will be your commanding officer for the rest of the term. Unfortunately, Mrs Chalkboard has hit some heavy weather and has had to take a spot of shore leave. So I'm depending on you all to help Mr Brainfright get his sea legs and learn the ropes. I'm sure if we all heave to and pull together we'll get the old tub through. Do I make myself clear?'

'Aye, aye, Principal Greenbeard,' we said.

Principal Greenbeard turned to Mr Brainfright

and saluted. 'Happy sailing, sir!' he said, and marched swiftly out of the room.

We stared at Mr Brainfright.

Mr Brainfright stared back at us, a wild gleam in his piercing green eyes.

Mr Brainfright was not like any other teacher I'd ever seen at Northwest Southeast Central School . . . and that's putting it mildly.

He was wearing a purple jacket, an orange shirt, and a bright green tie.

His hair darted out of his head in all sorts of crazy directions as if moments before stepping into our classroom he'd suffered a severe electric shock.

Plus he had that wild gleam in his eyes.

Mr Brainfright rubbed his hands together and smiled at us. 'Well, Class 5C,' he said. 'What are you going to teach me this morning?'

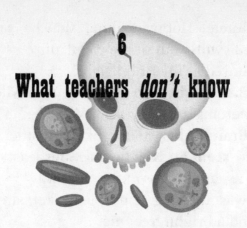

6
What teachers *don't* know

Now I don't know what the teachers at your school are like, but none of the teachers at Northwest Southeast Central have *ever* begun a lesson by asking us—the students—what *we* were going to teach *them*.

As we were about to find out, Mr Brainfright did things a little differently to other teachers.

Well, a *lot* differently, in fact.

'But you're supposed to teach *us*!' said Fiona.

'Where on earth did you get that idea?' said Mr Brainfright.

'Well, it's obvious,' said Fiona. 'You're the teacher!'

Mr Brainfright smiled. 'And you think teachers know everything?'

'Well, yes,' said Fiona.

Mr Brainfright stared at her. '*Every*thing?' he said.

'Well, no, not *every*thing,' said Fiona. 'But they are supposed to know more than the students.'

'I wouldn't be so sure of that,' said Mr Brainfright. 'Who can tell me something you know that I don't?'

'Our names!' said Jack, always quick off the mark. 'You don't know them and we do.'

Mr Brainfright nodded. 'Correct! Give me another one.'

'How to jump down a set of stairs on a skateboard without falling off,' said Gretel.

'Well, actually, I *can* do that,' said Mr Brainfright. 'But I have yet to master the handrail-slide . . . so, yes, your point still stands. There is still much I have to learn about skating the board. Another!'

'I bet you don't know how to groom a horse!' said Gina.

'Excellent!' said Mr Brainfright. 'You've got me there. I wouldn't even know which end of the horse to start at!'

'Oh, that's easy,' said Penny. 'The head, of course. You get a currycomb and—' Before she could continue, she was interrupted by Clive, which was a lucky thing because when Gina or Penny start talking about horses they can go on for a long time.

'You don't know how to make super-strength spitballs!' said Clive.

'Got me again,' said Mr Brainfright. 'It is an art of which I am sadly and woefully ignorant.'

Clive looked confused. I don't think he understood what Mr Brainfright was saying. But then, he doesn't understand much, apart from making super-strength spitballs and threatening people with his brother.

'How to fly!' said Grant.

'That's true,' said Mr Brainfright. 'I *don't* know how to fly. But I suspect that you don't either.'

'Not yet,' said Grant. 'But my dad is an inventor and he's working on a jet-propulsion unit small enough to fit in the heel of a shoe, and when it's ready he said I could be the first to use it.'

'Good for you!' said Mr Brainfright. 'I do hope you'll let me have a turn. I've always wanted to fly.'

'Sure,' said Grant. 'I'll talk to my dad.'

'So there you are!' said Mr Brainfright. 'You all have so much to teach me! The problem is, where do we start?'

'With maths!' said Fiona. 'We always study maths on Monday morning.'

'We'll get around to that a bit later,' said Mr Brainfright. 'But to begin with I'd like to start with the basics. First we are going to learn how to breathe.'

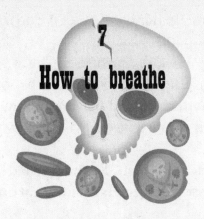

7
How to breathe

'But we already know how to breathe!' said David.

'Correction!' said Mr Brainfright. 'Most people *think* they know how to breathe, but they actually don't know the first thing about it.'

Mr Brainfright walked over to the bank of windows that ran along one side of the classroom and flung each of them wide open.

'Can anybody tell me what this is?' he said.

'A window?' said Jenny.

'Yes, and what else?' said Mr Brainfright.

'An open window?' said Jenny.

'And?' said Mr Brainfright, staring at each of us. 'And . . . ?'

Nobody was quite sure what to say. We all stared back at him.

'FRESH AIR!' he yelled.

Mr Brainfright was the first person I'd ever seen get *that* excited about fresh air.

Fiona put up her hand. 'Can we do maths now?' she said.

'But we haven't learned to *breathe* yet!' said Mr Brainfright. 'We can't do maths, or anything for that matter, if we don't know how to fill our brains with fresh oxygen. Now, everybody stand up, please.'

I rose to my feet. I'd never had a 'how to breathe' lesson before. Especially not on a Monday morning.

Monday mornings were normally spent arranging numbers in columns and adding, subtracting, multiplying and dividing them. Of course, you had to breathe while doing this, but breathing wasn't the point of the exercise. The point of the exercise was to get the right answer.

'All right,' said Mr Brainfright. 'Stand up straight. Place your hands on your stomach. Now take a deep breath in through your nose. Keep breathing in . . . your stomach should inflate like a small balloon.'

Fiona McBrain put up her hand. 'Will we be tested on this, sir?' she said.

'Tested?' said Mr Brainfright. 'What on earth are you talking about?'

'Normally Mrs Chalkboard tests us at the end of each new unit of work,' said Fiona.

'Would you like to be tested?' said Mr Brainfright.

'Yes!' said Fiona. 'I love tests!'

'Okay,' said Mr Brainfright. 'That's good. Because this is the most important test you will *ever* take. If you breathe correctly, you will live. If you don't, then . . . well . . . I'm afraid you won't be taking any more tests, on this or any other subject.'

Fiona nodded seriously. She had never failed a test in her life, and she wasn't about to start now. Especially when the stakes were so high.

Jenny nudged me and nodded in Newton's direction.

I looked over.

Newton was trembling.

'It's okay, Newton,' I whispered. 'Just keep breathing and you'll pass!'

Newton nodded.

'No whispering,' said Mr Brainfright. 'Just breathing!'

I breathed in. I felt my chest expand.

'As you breathe, feel the air as it enters your nostrils,' he said. 'Feel it as it passes across the back of your throat and down into your chest. Notice the moment where your lungs are full and that moment of stillness just before you breathe out again. Feel the oxygen from the air mixing with your blood. Feel your blood travelling to your arms, your legs and your brain. ISN'T BREATHING EXCITING?!'

'Can we sit down now?' said Clive.

'Sit down?' said Mr Brainfright. 'But we've only just started!'

David put up his hand. 'When are we going to start proper work, sir?' he said.

'This *is* proper work!' said Mr Brainfright, smiling. 'What could be more proper or important than learning how to breathe? You have to do it every day, every minute, every second that you are alive and if you were to stop you would die. I think it's worth a little bit of our attention, don't you?'

'But I like maths!' said Fiona. 'Can I count the number of breaths I take?'

'If you must,' said Mr Brainfright. 'But I don't see why just breathing isn't enough fun for you. I love breathing. The more fresh air the better!'

And saying that, Mr Brainfright stuck his head, and then the entire top half of his body, out the window.

'Breathe in,' he shouted, 'like so!'

I could see Mr Brainfright's chest expand, and then, suddenly, Mr Brainfright disappeared.

I blinked.

I couldn't quite believe it.

Mr Brainfright had fallen out the window!

Yes, you read that last sentence correctly.

MR BRAINFRIGHT HAD FALLEN OUT THE WINDOW!!!

I'm still not quite sure how it happened.
But it did.
It really did.

8
Class 5C to the rescue

Now you might be thinking, *No big deal, teachers at our school fall out the window all the time. Sometimes they're even pushed.* But what you don't know is that our classroom is on the second floor. If a teacher falls out *our* window, it's serious!

'Somebody *do* something!' said David.

'Why don't *you* do something?' said Jack. 'You're a class captain.'

'What do you suggest?' said David. 'This isn't exactly covered in the class captain's manual.'

'There's a class captain's manual?' said Jack. 'Really?'

'No, of course not!' said David. 'I was joking.'

'G-g-g-g . . .' said Newton.

'Uh-oh,' said Jenny. 'Newton's having another panic attack.'

'G-g-grab his feet!' said Newton, pointing to the window.

I rushed to the window.

Sure enough, just at the edge of the window sill, were two black tips—the tips of Mr Brainfright's shoes.

Mr Brainfright was hanging upside down by only his toes from a second-floor classroom window!

'I don't suppose you could give me a lift up, could you?' He said this very calmly and coolly, as if he wasn't hanging upside down by only his toes from a second-floor classroom window.

'Yes, sir,' I said. 'No problem.'

I grabbed one of Mr Brainfright's ankles and tried to pull him in, but he was too heavy. I turned around to face the class. They were all staring blankly at me.

'What are you waiting for?' I shouted. 'Give me a hand!'

Gretel Armstrong rushed over and grabbed Mr Brainfright's other ankle. 'Got you!' she said.

Gretel was so strong it was rumoured she could knock a person out with just one punch. Not that we'd ever seen her do it, but that was the rumour and nobody really wanted to test it to see whether or not it was true.

'What do we do now?' I said.

'Pull him in, of course!' said Gretel. 'Are you ready?'

I nodded. 'Ready! One, two, three, lift!'

Gretel and I lifted with every last bit of strength we had. But Mr Brainfright was still too heavy.

'We need backup!' said Gretel. 'Jenny! Put your arms around my waist. Then someone behind her, and someone behind them! David, you organise the boys to do the same around Henry's waist. When I give the signal we're all going to pull, got it?'

'Got it!' said Jenny.

'Brilliant!' said David. 'Why didn't I think of that?'

'Probably because it wasn't in the class captain's manual,' said Jack.

'Very funny, Jack,' said David. 'Now get into position. This is serious.'

'Aye, aye, captain,' said Jack, saluting David.

Once everyone had taken their place in line Gretel gave the order to pull.

'All right, everybody,' she said. 'Heave!'

'HEAVE!' yelled the class in response as we heaved.

'Heave!' said Gretel.

'HEAVE!' we yelled.

This went on for quite some time until slowly, but surely, we had pulled the bottom half of Mr Brainfright back into the room.

That's when the door of the classroom burst open.

9
Mrs Cross

'Just what do you think you are doing?' said a cross voice. The voice was so cross that it could only belong to one person: Mrs Cross. Mrs Cross was easily the crossest teacher at Northwest Southeast Central School. In fact, I don't think I'd ever seen Mrs Cross when she wasn't cross.

I glanced over my shoulder.

Mrs Cross was standing just inside the door, her face red and her hands on her hips.

'I'm trying to teach a lesson next door!' she said. 'But I can hardly hear myself speak for all the shouting in here! Would you please explain what on earth you are doing? And where is your teacher?'

Unfortunately—or fortunately, depending on how you want to look at it—at that very moment we were suddenly successful in pulling the top half of Mr Brainfright back into the classroom.

It was so sudden, however, that none of us were prepared and we all heaved backwards and fell sprawling on the floor around Mrs Cross's feet, causing her to fall over as well.

'Get off me!' said Mrs Cross, crossly pushing Fiona McBrain away. She stood up and brushed down her dress.

'Good morning,' said Mr Brainfright, very politely, as if he hadn't been hanging by his toes from a second-floor window only moments before. 'My name is Mr Brainfright. So sorry about the noise. I had a little accident.'

Mrs Cross glared at Mr Brainfright. 'Where is Mrs Chalkboard?'

'She's had to take a spot of shore leave,' said Mr Brainfright. 'I'm 5C's substitute teacher.'

'Is that so?' said Mrs Cross, eyeing him suspiciously. 'Well, could you keep the noise down? Some of us are trying to teach!'

'And some of us are falling out windows!' said Mr Brainfright.

Mrs Cross opened her mouth to speak but closed it again. Then, shaking her head, she turned and walked out of the classroom.

'Thank you for your assistance, everyone,' said Mr Brainfright. 'You may all return to your seats.'

I loved that.

We'd just saved his life and he 'thanked us for

our assistance' as if we'd done no more than hold the door open for him.

We went back to our seats and sat and stared at Mr Brainfright.

'As you can see,' he said, 'when you're breathing, it's very important not to fall out the window.'

10
Mr Brainfright's important lesson no. 1

When you're breathing, it's very important not to fall out the window.

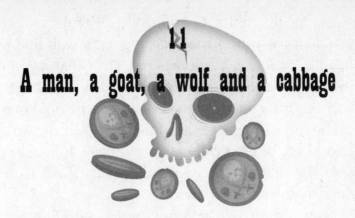

11
A man, a goat, a wolf and a cabbage

'Can we do maths now?' said Fiona.

The class groaned.

'Of course we can,' said Mr Brainfright.

The class groaned again.

'We're up to chapter ten in the book,' said Fiona helpfully.

'Which book is that?' said Mr Brainfright.

'*This* book,' said Fiona, holding up our class textbook, *Maths is Fun*.

Mr Brainfright took the book from Fiona and flipped through it. 'Hmmm,' he said. 'It says maths is fun, but you'd never suspect it from looking at this book, would you?'

'I like it,' said Fiona.

'What do you like about it particularly?' said Mr Brainfright.

'I like solving problems,' said Fiona.

'Solving problems, eh?' said Mr Brainfright,

stroking his chin thoughtfully. 'Here's a *real* problem for you! A man has a goat, a wolf and a head of cabbage. He comes to a river that has no bridge, but there is a small boat he can use to get across. Unfortunately, the boat can only hold one of the three things he has. If he takes over the wolf first, then the goat will eat the cabbage. If he takes over the cabbage, the wolf will eat the goat. How does he solve the problem?'

'But . . . but . . . that's not maths!' said Fiona.

'Why not?' said Mr Brainfright.

'Because it doesn't have any numbers!' said Fiona.

'It may not have numbers,' said Mr Brainfright, 'but it is definitely a problem. A real-life problem that all of you may well face in your own lives one day.'

'But I don't have a boat,' said David. 'Or a goat. Or a wolf. And I don't like cabbage, so why would I be carrying one around?'

'Use your imagination, David,' said Mr Brainfright.

'But you said it was a real-life problem,' said David.

'Imagination *is* real life,' said Mr Brainfright. 'And real life sometimes requires a great deal of imagination!'

'Why does this guy need to get across the river anyway?' said Clive.

'Not important,' said Mr Brainfright. 'But since you ask, let's say he's going to visit his friend who lives on the other side of the river.'

'Why does he have to take his goat and his wolf and a cabbage?' said Clive.

'Again, not important,' said Mr Brainfright. 'But perhaps he's worried they'll be lonely if he leaves them at home.'

'I understand how a wolf and a goat might be lonely,' said David, 'but how can a cabbage be lonely? Cabbages don't have feelings!'

'How can you be sure of that?' said Mr Brainfright.

'Because it's a CABBAGE!' said Fiona. 'Cabbages are plants, and plants don't have feelings!'

'This one does,' said Mr Brainfright. 'It's an unusually sensitive cabbage. It goes everywhere with the man. In fact, it's his best friend. He rescued it from a greengrocer one day. He heard it calling to him, "Help, help, they're going to eat me!" And the man quickly bought it, took it home, and the two became fast friends. So you see that there really was no question of the man leaving it at home, or risking it being eaten by the goat.'

Fiona and David sat there frowning.

'So there's the problem,' said Mr Brainfright. 'Who can suggest a solution?'

Clive put up his hand. 'If I was the man, I'd

strangle the wolf so it couldn't eat the goat and I'd strangle the goat so that it couldn't eat the cabbage. And then I'd strangle the cabbage so that it couldn't eat the goat or the wolf. And then it wouldn't matter which order I took them across the river.'

'But they'd all be dead!' I said.

'So?' said Clive.

'Well, it doesn't make any sense,' said Fiona. 'Why would the man strangle a cabbage? Cabbages don't eat wolves or goats.'

'Because the cabbage was going to strangle him!' said Clive. 'It was a bad cabbage.'

'But it's his best friend!' said Jenny.

'They'd had a fight,' said Clive.

Mr Brainfright looked at Clive and nodded. 'Interesting,' he said. 'Very interesting. But I think it would be preferable if he got them all across the river alive. Even the cabbage.'

'Suit yourself,' said Clive. 'I'm just trying to be helpful.'

'What sort of boat is it?' said Grant. 'Is it a speedboat?'

'No,' said Mr Brainfright.

'A powerboat?' said Grant. 'Powerboats are cool!'

'No,' said Mr Brainfright.

'A hovercraft?' said Grant hopefully. 'Hovercrafts are even cooler than powerboats!'

'It's not a hovercraft or a powerboat or a speedboat,' said Mr Brainfright. 'It's just a regular rowboat.'

'Oh,' said Grant, shrugging. 'Rowboats are *so* last century.'

'Does the man have a horse?' said Penny.

'No,' said Mr Brainfright. 'Just a wolf and a goat and a cabbage.'

'Where's his horse?' said Gina.

'I don't know,' said Mr Brainfright. 'Maybe it ran away.'

The twins looked alarmed. 'It ran away?' said Gina. 'Shouldn't he be trying to find it?'

'He is,' said Mr Brainfright, taking a deep breath. 'That's one of the reasons that he's crossing the river. To look for his horse.'

'But how did the horse cross the river?' said Gina.

'It's not important,' said Mr Brainfright. 'For all I know it rowed across in the boat!'

'No,' said Penny. 'Impossible. Horses can't row.'

'This one could,' said Mr Brainfright. 'But that's not important. What *is* important is how the man is going to get across the river with the wolf and the goat and the cabbage. First to suggest a solution gets a lollipop!'

That sure got everybody's attention. Nobody

really cared about goats, wolves or cabbages, but we *did* care about lollipops.

And nobody cared more about lollipops than me.

12
The exact number of people in the world who care more about lollipops than me

Zero.

13
A small wet blob

My problem was that I didn't know how to begin solving the problem.

Should the man take the cabbage across first? It was his best friend, after all. But while he was doing that, the wolf would eat the goat.

So it would obviously be better if the man took the wolf across first. But then the goat would eat the unguarded cabbage.

So it would be better if the man took the goat across first. But then the man would have to come back and get either the wolf or the cabbage, and if he took the wolf across, then it would eat the goat while he went back for the cabbage.

If he took the cabbage across, then the goat would eat the cabbage while he went back for the wolf.

It was impossible! There was no way the man could do it!

Suddenly ... *splat!* ... a small wet blob smacked into the back of my neck.

Now I had a new problem.

Clive Durkin.

Clive was not only the sort of person who would not hesitate to strangle wolves, goats and cabbages if he needed to get across a river in a hurry, but, as I think I've already mentioned, he also liked to chew up small pieces of paper, roll them into balls, and flick them at people.

And he'd chosen this moment to turn his attention to me.

I turned around. 'Very funny!' I said.

'What are you talking about?' said Clive, looking as innocent as he could, which wasn't very innocent at all. 'I didn't do anything!'

'Then what's this?' I said, picking the wet blob off the back of my neck.

'Beats me,' shrugged Clive, peering at the blob. 'Your brain?'

I was about to say something really funny back, like, 'No, I think it's *yours*,' but then I remembered the lollipop. I couldn't afford to get distracted. I had to be grown-up about this.

'Oh,' I said, looking at the blob. 'I wondered where it had got to. Thanks, Clive!'

That sure stopped him dead in his tracks.

I put the small piece of chewed-up paper

at the front of my desk and turned back to the problem.

But before I could even begin to consider whether the man with the boat should give up, go home, and maybe catch up with his friend by telephone, I felt another wet blob hit the back of my neck.

'Huh-huh-huh,' chuckled Clive. 'Gotcha again, McThrottle.'

I was tempted to remove the blob, turn around, and shove it up his nose, but I didn't have the time. I had a lollipop to win.

I picked the blob off the back of my neck, put it beside the first blob, and turned my attention back to the problem.

I felt another wet blob.

Then another.

I put the new blobs beside the first two blobs and studied them.

Four blobs.

I kept studying them. Four blobs . . . four blobs . . . just like the problem Mr Brainfright had set us: four things . . . a man, a goat, a wolf and a cabbage.

I took a deep breath as I realised that the blobs could stand in for the man, the goat, the wolf and the cabbage, and might actually help me solve the problem.

I glanced around the class. Nobody had figured it out yet. Not even Fiona or David. I still had a chance.

I arranged the blobs on one side of my desk. I placed my ruler in the centre to represent the river and then, using my eraser as a boat, I put the biggest blob on top of it.

I studied my eraser boat with the man-blob on top. What if the man left the cabbage with the wolf and took the goat across first? The cabbage-blob would be safe with the wolf-blob.

I placed the goat-blob onto the eraser boat and pushed it across the ruler river. The man-blob put the goat-blob onto the other side and then crossed the ruler river back to where the wolf-blob and cabbage-blob were waiting.

I studied my blobs. I couldn't take the wolf-blob across and leave it with the goat-blob . . . and I couldn't take the cabbage-blob across and leave it with the goat-blob . . . but who said I had to leave the goat-blob there?

In an instant I saw the solution. When you blobbed it out, it was obvious!

14
A solution

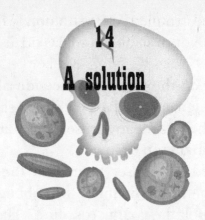

I was just about to put up my hand when David's hand shot up into the air first.

I couldn't believe it.

All that work!

All those blobs!

All for nothing!

'Yes?' said Mr Brainfright. 'Do you know the answer?'

'Not yet, sir,' said David. 'May I have permission to go to the bathroom?'

'Very well,' said Mr Brainfright.

The lollipop could still be mine!

But just then Jenny's hand shot into the air.

'I have the answer!' she said.

'Go ahead,' said Mr Brainfright.

'My mum always says there is no problem that can't be solved by people just sitting down and talking it over,' said Jenny. 'So if the man sits them all down and explains the situation and asks the goat not to eat the cabbage and asks the wolf not to eat the goat, then he can just take them all across in any order he wants.' Jenny smiled sweetly at Mr Brainfright. 'Do I get the lollipop?'

'No, I'm afraid not,' said Mr Brainfright.

'Why not?' said Jenny.

'Because your solution doesn't work,' said Mr Brainfright. 'The goat and the wolf can't talk.'

'But the cabbage can!' said Fiona.

'Yes,' said Mr Brainfright, 'that's because it's a *talking* cabbage.'

'But if cabbages can talk, why can't wolves and goats?' said Fiona.

'Some wolves and goats can talk,' said Mr Brainfright. 'But not these ones.'

'Oh, this is ridiculous!' said Fiona crossly.

'Ridiculous, maybe,' said Mr Brainfright. 'But not impossible. Does anybody else have a solution?'

I put up my hand.

Clive leaned forward. 'If you're thinking of telling on me, then think again!' he hissed. 'I'll tell Mr Brainfright I didn't do it!'

I just smiled.

Mr Brainfright looked at me. 'Do you have a solution for us?'

'Yes,' I said. 'What if the man took the goat

across first, and then went back for the cabbage and took that across and left the cabbage there, but then took the goat back and left it there while he took the wolf across, and left the wolf with the cabbage while he went back to get the goat?'

Mr Brainfright beamed. 'Perfect!' he said. 'What's your name, young man?'

'Henry,' I said. 'Henry McThrottle.'

'Well, Henry McThrottle,' said Mr Brainfright, 'you just earned yourself a lollipop. Come up to the front.'

'Well done, Henry!' said Jenny, as I got up.

I walked to Mr Brainfright's desk. Mr Brainfright opened a battered crimson briefcase, produced a large red lollipop, and put it into my hand.

As I walked back to my desk, I made a point of waving my lollipop at Clive. 'Thanks for the blobs,' I whispered. 'I couldn't have solved the problem without them.'

Clive just stared at me. He wasn't laughing anymore.

As I sat down, Fiona put up her hand. 'Will we be tested on this, sir?' she said.

15
Fred Durkin

Before Mr Brainfright could answer Fiona, the lunch bell rang and everybody stood up and headed outside.

It was warm and sunny out in the yard.

I was feeling good. Not only did we have a very interesting new teacher, but I had a lollipop to eat for lunch. That beat a cheese sandwich any day.

I was halfway across the yard, though, when two things happened.

The first was that a dark grey cloud passed in front of the sun.

The second was that Fred and Clive Durkin appeared in front of me.

'Hand over the lollipop, McThrottle,' said Fred, his hand outstretched.

'But it's *mine*,' I said.

'That's not what my brother tells me,' said Fred.

'He said you won the lollipop using spitballs that he made.'

'Yes,' I said, 'that's true, but I didn't ask him to fire spitballs at me.'

'Nevertheless you used *his* spitballs, so hand over the lollipop,' said Fred.

'No,' I said. I started walking away.

But before I could get very far, I felt a big hand on my shoulder. It spun me around. Fred reached out and snatched the lollipop from me.

'Hey!' I said, lunging forward to grab my lollipop.

As I did, Clive stuck his leg out in front of me.

Instead of lunging forward, I tripped forward and collapsed on top of Fred. Not very pleasant for me, but even less pleasant for him.

My fingers were getting closer and closer to the lollipop. And then I felt my entire body being lifted up in the air.

'McThrottle!' said an angry voice. 'What is the meaning of this?'

My feet touched the ground. I was standing in front of Mrs Cross, who was in an even crosser mood than usual. If there was one thing that made her crosser than anything else, it was catching students fighting in the yard while she was on yard duty.

'Well?' she said, staring at me. 'Why are you attacking poor Fred?'

I looked at Fred lying on the ground, writhing around as if he was in agony. What an actor! If only the teachers knew what he was *really* like. He was completely different when they were around.

'He's a thief!' I said. 'He stole my lollipop!'

'No, I never,' said Fred, who had such a pained look on his face that you would have sworn he was speaking with his dying breath. 'It was *my* lollipop!'

'He's right,' said Clive. 'It was definitely his lollipop.'

Mrs Cross shook her head. 'Henry, this is not the Northwest Southeast Central School way! It makes me very cross when Northwest Southeast Central School students steal each other's food and fight like animals in the yard! This is completely unacceptable!'

'But I didn't do anything!' I said.

'You didn't do anything?' she said. 'So are you telling me that there's something wrong with my eyes? Are you telling me that I didn't just see you attacking Fred Durkin?'

'He attacked me first,' I said. 'He attacked me and stole my lollipop!'

'That's quite enough,' said Mrs Cross. 'Go and wait outside Principal Greenbeard's office. I'll let him know to expect you. Clive, help me get Fred

43

to the sick bay. We'll be lucky if he doesn't need an ambulance after such a brutal attack!'

'But . . .' I said, breathless with the injustice of it all, '. . . but . . .'

'Not another word!' said Mrs Cross. 'Go straight to Principal Greenbeard's office!'

I shook my head and trudged off towards the admin building. I walked as slowly as I could. Of course, if I'd known what I was about to find out in Principal Greenbeard's office, I would have run to get there.

16
Mrs Rosethorn

I walked slowly to the main office and took a deep breath, trying to make myself feel brave, before entering the reception area. I wasn't scared of the principal—he was harmless enough—but I was scared of the receptionist, Mrs Rosethorn. As I took a seat on the bench, I could feel her disapproving glare burning into me.

Mrs Rosethorn was terrifying.

And she didn't like time wasters. And just in case you forgot, there was a sign pasted on the glass that said NO TIME WASTERS.

If you went up to the office window you had to state your business quickly and clearly. The difficulty was that when Mrs Rosethorn looked at you, her glare was so intense that you found yourself stunned and unable to remember why you were there.

'Yes?' said Mrs Rosethorn now, sliding open the

window and glaring at me. Her eyes were like twin laser beams shooting into my brain and erasing all my thoughts.

I, of course, immediately forgot why I was there.

'Um . . .' I stammered, 'M-M-Mrs Cross . . .'

'Mrs Cross?' said Mrs Rosethorn. 'What about Mrs Cross? Hurry up, boy! No time wasting! Spit it out! I haven't got all day, you know!'

'I know,' I said. 'I-I'm very sorry, Mrs Rosethorn . . . I-I . . .'

'Oh for goodness' sake!' said Mrs Rosethorn. 'Let me guess—Mrs Cross has caught you up to no good in the yard and sent you to see Principal Greenbeard. Is that it?'

I nodded.

'I'll let him know you're here,' she said, glaring at me. 'Meanwhile, sit down on the bench and stay out of trouble!'

Mrs Rosethorn picked up the telephone, keeping her eyes on me the whole time. I shrank back into the bench. 'He'll see you now,' she said, hanging up the telephone. 'Look smart!'

I got up, tucked in my shirt, and knocked on the door.

'Come aboard!' a voice cried.

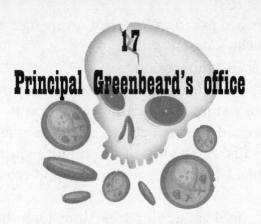

17
Principal Greenbeard's office

I entered, stood to attention and saluted.

Principal Greenbeard was sitting at his desk with a small tube of glue in his hand. In front of him was a model of a Spanish galleon. I knew this because Principal Greenbeard had taught us a whole unit of work on different types of ships. I was soon to wish that I'd paid more attention.

'At ease, sailor,' said Principal Greenbeard. 'Mrs Cross called from the sick bay and told me to expect you. Have a seat.'

I took a seat in front of his desk and looked around the office. The walls were covered with framed paintings of ships. There was a mariner's signal flag mounted above the window behind Principal Greenbeard. And in a glass-fronted cabinet there was a pair of antique pistols in a velvet-lined case.

'Do you know what this is, Henry?' Principal

Greenbeard asked as he glued a tiny figure to the ship's crow's nest.

'A pirate ship?' I said.

'Yes,' said Principal Greenbeard. 'But not just any pirate ship. Do you know *which* pirate ship?'

I studied the model. It had three masts and many sails. At the top of the middle mast was a small black flag with a white skull and crossbones on it.

'No, sir,' I said. 'All pirate ships look the same to me.'

Principal Greenbeard raised his bushy black eyebrows. 'Well, they're not!' he said. 'This is Blackbeard's ship. The *Queen Anne's Revenge*! You've heard of Blackbeard the pirate, I assume?'

'Yes, sir,' I said.

'Do you know what Blackbeard would do to members of his crew who failed to follow orders?'

'No, sir.'

'Well let me tell you,' he said. 'Blackbeard would blindfold them, tie their hands behind their back, and then make them walk out onto a plank attached to the side of the ship, poking them all the while in the backside with the sharp end of a cutlass. Then, when they reached the end of the plank, they'd fall off into the sea and be eaten by hungry sharks! What do you think of that, Henry?'

I shook my head. 'I don't think it sounds too good, sir.'

'Not too good at all!' said Principal Greenbeard, carefully pushing his model aside so that he could lean forward on his desk and fix me with a terrifying stare. 'So if you were a crew member on Blackbeard's ship, it would be best to keep your nose clean and stay out of trouble. Wouldn't it, Henry?'

'Yes, Principal Greenbeard.'

'Unless you wanted to be blindfolded, poked in the backside with a cutlass, made to walk the plank, and eaten alive by sharks, that is. You don't want to be eaten alive by sharks, do you, Henry?'

I felt it was a rather unnecessary question, but Principal Greenbeard seemed to be waiting for an answer.

'No, sir,' I said, checking the office for a tank of hungry sharks with a plank mounted above it. It would not have surprised me to see one.

'You know, Henry,' said Principal Greenbeard, 'I run a tight ship here. And it's my job to protect that ship and all who sail in her from dangers, both from without and within.'

'Yes, Principal Greenbeard,' I said.

'I need my crew to pull together!' he said, warming to his subject. 'All hands on deck!'

'Yes, Principal Greenbeard.'

'We're on a grand adventure, Henry. Let's not ruin it by fighting amongst ourselves like a pack of scurvy dogs!'

'No, sir.' I wasn't exactly sure what a 'scurvy dog' was. Maybe he was referring to Thief. Thief is a stray dog that hangs around the school and steals lunch bags from the lockers if they're not closed properly.

'Mrs Cross tells me you attacked Fred Durkin,' said Principal Greenbeard. 'What do you have to say for yourself?'

'I didn't attack Fred,' I said. 'Not on purpose, anyway.'

'How do you attack someone accidentally?' asked Principal Greenbeard.

I told him the whole story. About how Mr Brainfright had set the problem of the man and the wolf and the goat and the cabbage and offered a lollipop as the prize and how much I loved lollipops and how much I wanted to win the lollipop and how I used the blobs to solve the problem and how I'd won the lollipop and how happy and excited I'd been to win the lollipop and how much I was looking forward to eating the lollipop and how upset I'd been when Fred snatched it out of my hand and how I'd tried to snatch it back but I'd tripped and fallen on top of him.

'Shiver me timbers, Henry, my boy!' said Principal Greenbeard. 'That's quite some story. I understand how you must feel. It's awful to have something precious stolen from you.'

'Yes, sir,' I nodded. 'It is.'

'I know, Henry. I know exactly what it's like because I, too, was once the victim of a terrible theft.'

'Really, sir?' I said.

'Yes,' he said. 'When I was your age, at this very school, my friends and I used to pretend that we were pirates. Can you imagine that, Henry? Pirates! Hard to believe, isn't it?'

Sitting there surrounded by model ships, flags and antique pistols, it wasn't too hard to believe at all, but I nodded anyway. 'Yes, sir.'

'We spent our lunchtimes sailing around the yard in an imaginary pirate ship,' said Principal Greenbeard. 'We even had our own chest of treasure, which we buried on Skull Island.'

'Buried treasure?' I said. He had my interest now.

'Yes,' said Principal Greenbeard. 'We filled that chest with the most valuable things that we could beg, buy, borrow and—I'm ashamed to admit it—steal. It was a treasure beyond compare, Henry, my boy. *Beyond compare!* We buried it on Skull Island . . . and then never saw it again.'

'What happened?' I said. 'Did you lose the map?'

'No,' said Principal Greenbeard, his eyes growing misty. 'We didn't lose the map. We dug up the treasure chest a week later and the chest was there all right, exactly where we buried it, but it was completely empty—except for a note . . .'

'What did the note say?'

Principal Greenbeard drew a deep breath. He reached across his desk, opened the lid of an old wooden box and removed a piece of notepaper. He unfolded it and began to read.

'Search the Northwest Southeast Central seas
Search upon bended and bloodied knees
But your treasure again you will never see
Your pirate gang is no match for me.

Dig for one thousand nights and a night
Dig for your treasure as much as you like
But of your riches you will only dream—
Greenbeard's pirates are no match for me.'

Principal Greenbeard put the paper down on the desk in front of me.

'So what did you do?' I asked.

'We searched, of course. It was clearly a challenge to us. We searched and dug up every square inch of the school.'

'But you didn't find it?'

'No,' said Principal Greenbeard. 'We never saw our treasure again.'

'Who do you think stole it?' I said.

Principal Greenbeard shrugged. 'It was obviously a rival pirate,' he said, 'but we never found out who. Our pirate treasure was stolen: by a pirate! We didn't play pirates anymore after that. It took all the fun out of it. As far as I'm concerned, Henry, piracy is just another word for theft.'

'Wow!' I said, trying to take it all in. 'Where is Skull Island exactly?'

'That's what we called the hill next to the sports field,' he said. 'But that's not the point . . .'

'And the treasure is still buried somewhere in the school?' I said.

'As far as I know,' said Principal Greenbeard sadly. 'But the details aren't important. All I know is that I never saw the treasure again. Upon my oath, Henry, how I hate pirates! I vowed that day that when I grew up I would be the principal of the school and I would use my powers to outlaw piracy and make sure no student ever had to suffer that sort of loss or disappointment again.'

'And you're *sure* they reburied it?' I said.

'As sure as any man can be about anything on this watery globe,' he said. 'But it doesn't matter now. What matters is that we put childish things behind us and all work together to make sure piracy never rears its ugly head at Northwest Southeast Central School ever again . . .'

Principal Greenbeard rambled on for some time about responsibility, maturity and scurvy dogs but, to tell you the truth, I couldn't really concentrate. I was too busy memorising that note and thinking about that long-lost treasure.

And about how I, Henry McThrottle, was going to find it.

18
Treasure!

As I left Principal Greenbeard's office, it seemed like I was stepping back into a different world from the one I'd left. The floor seemed shinier than before. The awards and sporting shields on the reception walls were sparkling as if they'd been freshly polished. And Mrs Rosethorn seemed softer and, well, almost *pleasant*.

'Make sure you shut the door on your way out, you little troublemaker!' she barked.

Well, I did say *almost* pleasant.

I closed the door and walked down the front steps. I still felt sad about the loss of my lollipop, but at the same time I couldn't help feeling excited about the possibility of finding buried treasure.

Jenny, Gretel and Newton were sitting under the trees on the far side of the basketball court. Jack was using a piece of chalk to redraw the court lines and mess up the basketball players—one of his favourite pastimes.

'Are you okay, Henry?' said Jenny. 'We heard you got sent to Principal Greenbeard's office.'

Newton whispered, 'What did you do?'

'I didn't do anything,' I said. 'Clive and Fred started a fight and Mrs Cross caught us and blamed me.'

'Typical!' said Gretel, smacking her fist into her palm. 'I ought to go sock that Fred Durkin in the mouth!'

'Me too!' said Jack, who had finished annoying the basketball players. 'And I'd come and help you . . . except that my hand is a little sore from all that drawing, and . . .'

'No,' I said. 'I don't want anybody socking anybody in the mouth. You see, Fred and Clive don't know it, but they did me a favour.'

Gretel frowned. 'Huh?'

'While I was in Principal Greenbeard's office I found out the most amazing thing!'

'That Principal Greenbeard's beard is fake?' said Gretel. 'I knew it!'

'No, not that,' I said. 'Something better!'

'That he wears a wig?' said Jenny.

'No,' I said. 'Even better!'

'I know!' said Jack. 'You saw top-secret plans for knocking the school down and replacing it with an amusement park.'

'No,' I said, 'even better than that!'

'Impossible!' said Jack. 'What could possibly be better than a plan to knock down the school and build an amusement park?'

'Buried treasure!' I said.

'Buried treasure?' Newton gasped. 'Where?'

'Skull Island,' I said.

'Skull Island?' said Jack. 'Isn't that where King Kong lives? In the South Pacific?'

'No,' I said. 'That's just in the movie.' I pointed at the small rounded hill in the middle of the yard. 'Our Skull Island is over there.'

'That's not an island,' said Jack. 'It's just a dumb old hill.'

'Maybe to you it is,' I said. 'But that's not how Principal Greenbeard and his friends saw it when they went to this school. They used to play pirates and that hill was their headquarters. They called it Skull Island. One day they buried a chest full of treasure on it, but when they went back to dig it up all they found was an empty chest and a note.'

'A note?' said Jenny. 'What did it say?'

I closed my eyes and began to recite the poem I'd memorised in Principal Greenbeard's office.

'Search the Northwest Southeast Central seas
Search upon bended and bloodied knees

But your treasure again you will never see
Your pirate gang is no match for me.

Dig for one thousand nights and a night
Dig for your treasure as much as you like
But of your riches you will only dream—
Greenbeard's pirates are no match for me.

'Principal Greenbeard and his friends searched
and searched but they never could find it. It's still
buried somewhere in the school grounds.'

'Wow!' said Newton. 'What do you suppose the
treasure is?'

'Gold, probably!' said Jack. 'And most likely
rubies, emeralds and diamonds!'

'Bracelets,' said Jenny. 'Strings of pearls!
Rings!'

'Don't forget jewel-encrusted daggers and
goblets,' said Gretel. 'Pirates love jewel-encrusted
daggers and goblets.'

'And pieces of eight,' said Newton. 'Lots and
lots of pieces of eight!'

'What are pieces of eight?' Jack asked.

'I don't know,' said Newton, 'but there are
probably lots of them.'

'One thing's for sure,' I said. 'Whatever is in that
chest must be pretty old by now, and old things
are worth a *lot* of money.'

'That's right,' said Jenny. 'My uncle found this really old coin and it turned out to be worth TWO THOUSAND DOLLARS.'

'Two thousand dollars?' said Jack. 'And that's just *one* coin! Do you suppose Greenbeard's treasure had coins in it?'

'He didn't say,' I said, 'but given how much pirates love coins, I'd say it's pretty likely.'

'Highly likely, I'd say,' said Gretel. 'And there's probably more than one rare coin. Probably *thousands*.'

'Hundreds of thousands,' said Newton.

'Maybe even millions!' said Jenny.

'Don't get carried away,' I said, but it was too late. They already had.

'Imagine how much fun you could have with a million dollars!' said Jack.

'You could have a huge party for all your friends!' said Jenny.

Gretel punched the air and whooped. 'All right! Can I come?'

'You're my friend, aren't you?' said Jenny.

'Yes, of course I am,' said Gretel.

'Then you're invited!' said Jenny.

'But *everyone's* your friend!' I said. 'You'd have to invite the whole school.'

'I don't see a problem with that,' said Jenny. 'We've got a million dollars . . . at least!'

'What about Clive Durkin?' said Jack. 'Would you invite him?'

'Yes,' said Jenny.

'But he's not your friend!' said Jack.

'Yes he is,' said Jenny. 'He just doesn't know it yet. And I'd have to invite him anyway because otherwise he'd tell his brother and his brother wouldn't like it.'

'Smart thinking,' said Gretel.

Newton was shifting around uncomfortably.

'What's the matter, Newton?' said Jenny.

'I don't want to be rich,' he said.

'Why not?'

'All that money . . .' said Newton. 'How would you keep it safe?'

'Put it in the bank, of course,' said Jack.

'How do you know the bank would keep it safe?' said Newton.

'Because that's what banks do,' said Jack. 'They keep money safe.'

'What about bank robbers?' said Newton. 'That's what they do—they rob banks!'

'Get a grip, Newton,' said Jack. 'We haven't even got the money yet and you're worrying about it being stolen!'

'Yeah, Jack's right,' I said. 'We haven't found the treasure yet. We need a plan.'

'I have a plan,' said Gretel. 'I say we start

looking for it right away,'

'Good plan, Gretel!' said Jenny.

'But what if people see us looking for it?' said Jack.

'Good point, Jack,' said Jenny.

'We'll tell them we're *not* looking for treasure,' said Newton.

'Great idea, Newton!' said Jenny.

'Newton's right,' I said. 'It's important that we keep this just between us. This is our secret. It's not our treasure until we actually find it. Repeat the oath after me: "Cross my heart, hope to die, stick a needle in my eye."'

Everyone repeated the oath, except for Newton, who got a bit freaked out by the bit about the needle. 'A needle?' he said. 'I don't want to stick a needle in my eye!'

'Well, don't say anything about the treasure and you won't have to,' said Jack.

'But what if I do it accidentally?' said Newton. 'What if I say something about the treasure in my sleep?'

'Do you talk in your sleep?' asked Jenny.

'I don't know,' said Newton. 'I'm asleep.'

'Don't worry about it then,' said Jenny. 'I'm sure you wouldn't have to stick a needle in your eye in that case, would he, Henry?'

'No,' I said. 'That would be okay.'

The bell for the end of lunch rang.

'We'll start the search tomorrow,' I said. 'And remember—this is our secret. Don't breathe a word to anyone.'

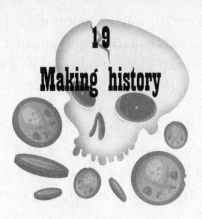

19
Making history

'Good morning, class,' said Mr Brainfright cheerfully.

'Good morning, Mr Brainfright,' we chanted back.

'And it *is* a good morning,' said Mr Brainfright. 'A particularly good morning to study history.'

The class groaned.

Maths was bad, but history was even worse. We'd been studying the history of Ancient Rome. Talk about tedious. Tedious maximus.

I'd tried to liven things up a bit by making a working model of the volcano that erupted and destroyed the city of Pompeii, but it hadn't worked out the way I'd planned.

I'd made the model volcano out of clay. It was hollow in the middle and to make real smoke and real flame, I'd stuffed it full of newspaper. When I lit it with a match during my class presentation, real smoke and real flame came out of it all right.

In fact so much smoke and flame came out that it set off the fire alarm and we'd had to evacuate the school until the fire brigade came and gave us the all-clear.

Mrs Chalkboard wouldn't let me make any more model volcanoes after that, so I'd sort of lost interest in history. I wasn't alone.

'Hands up if you don't like history,' said Mr Brainfright.

Everybody put up their hands.

Well, everybody except Fiona McBrain—but that was predictable. Fiona McBrain was interested in practically everything. So am I, actually—the difference is that I am only interested in *interesting* things. She was interested in boring things as well.

'Okay,' said Mr Brainfright. 'Looks like we're outnumbered, Fiona. Who can tell me what's wrong with history?'

'It's boring,' said Jack. 'It's about boring old people who lived thousands of years ago and it's got nothing to do with us.'

'That's where you're wrong,' said Mr Brainfright. 'It's got *everything* to do with us. History isn't confined to thousands of years ago. It's happening all the time!'

'How do you figure that?' said Jack.

'Well,' said Mr Brainfright, 'what did you have for breakfast this morning?'

'Um . . . cornflakes,' said Jack.

'That's history!' said Mr Brainfright.

'No it's not,' argued Jack. 'It was just a bowl of cornflakes.'

'It's still history,' said Mr Brainfright. 'It happened in the past and you're not a boring old person who lived thousands of years ago.'

'Wow,' said Jack. 'So this morning I made history.'

'Not just you, Jack,' said Mr Brainfright. 'We *all* made history today. In fact, we are making history all the time. We couldn't stop making history if we tried, because even if we tried to stop making history the very fact that we tried to stop making history would become the history that we were trying not to make.'

Mr Brainfright paused, breathless with the excitement of his history-making speech.

'And not just this morning, either,' he said. 'Your whole lives have been full of historical moments—moments that have never existed on Earth in quite the same way before and never will again.'

'So when I cut my finger on the bread knife this morning,' said Jenny, 'that was history?'

'Yes!' said Mr Brainfright. 'History! Who else has a historical moment that they can share?'

'When my dad was helping me with my new chemistry set and we blew the roof off his workshop!' said Grant.

The class laughed.

'History again!' said Mr Brainfright.

I thought of Principal Greenbeard as a kid, hiding his treasure. That was history, too.

'Will we be tested on this, sir?' said Fiona, who was furiously taking notes, just in case.

'Who can say what's going to happen next?' said Mr Brainfright. 'I don't know, but I can't wait to find out! Does anybody else have any historical moments for us?'

'When I had a spider in my bedroom and my mum stood on a chair and tried to catch it in a glass but one of its legs was too long and it got cut off and fell onto the carpet and it *wriggled*,' said Newton.

The whole class let out a squeal of disgust.

'When you fell out the window yesterday during our "how to breathe" lesson,' I said.

'Now that's what I call history!' said Mr Brainfright. 'Who knows? In two thousand years students might be studying my fall out the window as part of their history class. They might even stage re-enactments!'

'Cool!' said Jack. 'I love re-enactments!'

'Me too!' said Gretel.

'So do I,' said Fiona, 'as long as they're historically accurate and not just an excuse to play dress-ups for the fun of it.'

'Life is an excuse to play dress-ups just for the fun of it, Fiona,' said Mr Brainfright. 'Hey, I've got a great idea. Why don't we stage a re-enactment of yesterday's fall right now? We're all wearing historically accurate costumes. It will be just like going back in a time machine!'

'I don't think that's such a good idea,' said David. 'You could have been seriously injured yesterday.'

'But I wasn't, was I?' said Mr Brainfright. 'Thanks to the quick thinking of the class. Okay, now where were we?'

'You were over by the window,' said Fiona, reading from her notes.

'About here?' said Mr Brainfright.

'A little bit more to the left,' said Fiona.

Mr Brainfright moved to the left. 'Like so?' he said.

'Yes,' said Fiona. 'And then you said, "But I don't see why just breathing isn't enough fun for you. I love breathing. The more fresh air the better!" After that, you stuck the top half of your body out the window.'

'Like this?' said Mr Brainfright, putting the whole top half of his body out the window.

'Yes,' said Fiona, 'just like that. And then

you said, "Breathe in . . . like so!" and—Mr Brainfright?'

But Mr Brainfright didn't respond. And there was a good reason for that. Mr Brainfright had just fallen out the window—again!

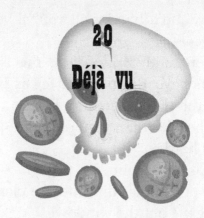

20
Déjà vu

For a moment the class was silent.

And then there was complete uproar.

Newton squealed.

'Déjà vu!' said Jack.

'You can say that again,' I said.

'Déjà vu!' said Jack.

'Stop being silly!' said Jenny. 'This is no joke!'

We ran to the window.

The toes of Mr Brainfright's shoes were in exactly the same place as yesterday.

I grabbed his left ankle.

'Gretel!' I yelled. 'Grab his other leg! David, put your arms around my waist. Everybody else take your positions exactly as you were yesterday!'

'I told him this would happen!' said David.

'That doesn't change the fact that it's happened!' I said.

'But I *did* warn him,' said David.

'Just give me a hand, will you?' I yelled. 'This is serious!'

'No,' shouted Mr Brainfright, 'this is history!'

I pulled on Mr Brainfright's leg as I waited for the rest of the class to get into place.

He felt heavier than yesterday.

I pulled harder.

But I was losing him.

Instead of pulling him into the classroom, he was pulling *me* out the window!

'Gretel!' I said. 'Help me!'

'I'm trying!' she said, but I could see the same thing was happening to her.

Slowly but surely we were *both* being pulled out the window . . . And then suddenly we weren't halfway out the window—we were *all* the way out the window!

I was upside down, face into the wall, hanging from the window ledge by my toes.

Gretel was beside me in exactly the same position.

We were both still holding onto Mr Brainfright's legs.

And then Mr Brainfright started laughing.

Now, I like Mr Brainfright.

I like him a lot.

But I was seriously starting to worry about his mental health.

'Are you feeling all right, Mr Brainfright?' I said.

'Never better!' he said.

And then the strangest thing happened.

Gretel and I started laughing as well.

I mean, don't get me wrong, it was a terrifying situation to be in, but his laughter was contagious.

Meanwhile, above us, I could hear the class arguing about what to do.

'I warned him!' David was saying. 'I warned them all!'

'Stop being such a know-it-all,' said Fiona.

'You should talk!' said David.

'I don't think this arguing is helping,' said Jenny. 'We should be working together to help them.'

'Wow!' said Jack. 'This is the best history lesson ever!'

'Hey!' I yelled, between giggles. 'If it's not too much trouble, could somebody actually *do* something?'

'What do you suggest?' called David. 'You're too heavy for us to pull in.'

'How about you get a video camera and film us for the funniest home video show?' said Gretel.

'No need to be sarcastic,' said David.

'I wasn't,' said Gretel. 'I love the funniest home video show and I've always wanted to be on it.'

'Get a ladder!' I yelled. 'Call the fire brigade! I don't care what! Get Grant to put his flying boots on!'

'They haven't been tested yet,' said Grant. 'It would be too dangerous.'

'No more dangerous than the situation we're already in!' I said.

'Then why are you laughing so much?' said Jenny.

'I don't know,' I said. 'Why are we laughing, Mr Brainfright?'

'Why not laugh?' said Mr Brainfright. 'We might as well enjoy ourselves.'

'But we could die!' said Gretel.

'All the more reason to enjoy ourselves while we still can!' said Mr Brainfright.

And then we fell.

21
Mr Spade

We fell and fell and fell.

We fell for what felt like a long time, but I now realise it was probably only about one second before we landed, all three of us, headfirst in the garden bed.

I was the first to pull my head out of the soft dirt.

The fact that all three of us had landed upside down in the garden bed did not escape the gardener's attention.

'GET OUT OF MY GARDEN!' yelled Mr Spade from the other side of the sports field.

He was running towards us with a pitchfork in his hand.

I pulled Gretel up out of the dirt.

'Quick, Gretel,' I said. 'We have to go. Give me a hand with Mr Brainfright!'

Mr Brainfright's head was still firmly planted in the soil.

We pulled him out.

Mr Brainfright shook the dirt from his head. He looked a little dazed, but all right.

Mr Spade was close.

'Run!' said Gretel.

Nobody was laughing now.

Hanging upside down from a second-storey window may have had its funny side, but there was nothing funny about the sight of Mr Spade's pitchfork.

Luckily, we were the faster runners.

We made it around the building and back up the steps into the corridor before he could catch us.

We entered the classroom to a huge cheer from the rest of the class.

'I can't believe you're still alive!' said Jenny, throwing her arms around me.

'Me neither!' I said.

Suddenly there was yelling in the corridor.

The door burst open.

This time it wasn't Mrs Cross.

It was worse.

It was Mr Spade!

'What do you mean by destroying my flowerbed?' he yelled.

'We couldn't help it,' said Mr Brainfright. 'We fell out the window and, well, there was nowhere else to land.'

'You fell out the window?' growled Mr Spade, shaking his head. 'How in the blazes do three people fall out a classroom window?'

'It was a historical re-enactment,' I started to explain. 'You see—'

'What is the meaning of all this shouting?' said Mrs Cross, who had just come into the room. 'I'm trying to teach a class!'

'Oh, hello, Mrs Cross,' said Mr Brainfright. 'We had a little accident.'

'They fell out the window!' said Mr Spade. 'Right into my freshly planted flowerbed.'

'Didn't you fall out the window yesterday?' said Mrs Cross.

'Yes,' said Mr Brainfright. 'As I said, just a little accident. Could have happened to anybody.'

'ONCE is an accident,' said Mrs Cross. 'TWICE is pure stupidity! In all my time at Northwest Southeast Central School I have never heard such a noisy, disruptive class as this one. Never!'

Mr Brainfright had a big smile on his face.

'Did you hear that, 5C?' he said. 'We just made history—again!'

'You'll be history, young man, if you can't keep your class quiet,' said Mrs Cross. 'You mark my words.'

And with that, she left the room, banging the door shut behind her.

Mr Brainfright turned and winked at us. 'I think she likes me!' he said.

'Well, I don't think she does,' said Mr Spade, pointing his pitchfork at Mr Brainfright, and then at us. 'And I don't like you either. Keep out of my flowerbeds. Or else.'

We all nodded.

Mr Spade stomped off down the corridor.

'Well, Jack,' said Mr Brainfright, 'history's not quite as boring as you thought, is it?'

'No, sir!' said Jack, grinning.

22
Mr Brainfright's important lesson no. 2

History is not quite as boring as you might think.

23
Skull Island

I enjoyed that lesson.

I enjoyed that lesson a lot.

Despite the fact that I had almost died, I enjoyed that lesson more than I'd enjoyed any lesson ever.

Mr Brainfright was not only a great history teacher, but a great history re-enactor as well.

But when the lunch bell rang, Jack, Gretel, Jenny, Newton and I still sprinted for the door. None of us bothered about lunch—we were all too eager to start searching for the buried treasure.

We ran down the steps, out into the yard and stood there blinking in the bright sunlight.

'Well, Henry,' said Jack. 'Where do we start?'

'Excellent question, Jack,' I said.

'What's the answer?' he said.

'I have no idea,' I admitted.

'We're going to have to split up,' said Gretel. 'Henry, you search the sports field. Jenny, you take the basketball courts. Jack can do the juniors' area, including the sandpit. Newton, you do the flowerbeds.'

'The flowerbeds?' said Newton, horrified. 'But what about Mr Spade?'

'What about Mr Spade?' said Gretel.

'He'll kill me if he finds me digging in the flowerbeds!'

'Good point,' said Gretel. 'We'll leave the flowerbeds until last. Meanwhile, you can help me do the front of the school. We meet back here in fifteen minutes. Okay?'

We all nodded and went to search our areas.

Fifteen minutes later we were all back in the same place blinking at each other in the bright sunlight.

'Well?' said Jack. 'Did anybody find it?'

I shook my head. Jenny shook her head. Gretel and Newton shook their heads.

'Me neither,' said Jack. 'What now?'

'The flowerbeds?' suggested Jenny.

'No,' said Newton. 'Too scary.'

'Forget the flowerbeds,' I said. 'If it was there Mr Spade would have found it by now. How about we go up to the top of Skull Island and look around? You can see the whole school from up there. Maybe that will give us a clue.'

'Great idea, Henry,' said Jenny. 'Let's go.'

We climbed to the top of Skull Island. Not only could we see clear across the school in all directions, we could also see right into Mrs Cross's classroom.

She was busily writing on the board.

'Doesn't she know it's lunchtime?' I said.

'I'm sure she does,' said Jenny. 'She's writing lines for the students she's held back.'

Jenny was right. At the back of the classroom were five students, and they all looked miserable.

At that moment, Fred Durkin came into the classroom and handed Mrs Cross a lunch bag. She smiled at him, put the bag on her desk and turned back to the board. Fred looked up and saw us. He poked out his tongue. Then he left the classroom.

'Look at him, sucking up to his teacher,' said Jack. 'Bringing her lunch while she keeps those poor kids in.'

'Makes you sick, doesn't it?' said Gretel. 'He's so two-faced.'

'Forget about Fred,' said Jenny. 'Let's get back to treasure hunting. Can anybody see a place where it might be buried?'

'It would have been found by now if we could *see* it,' Jack pointed out.

'Did Principal Greenbeard say anything about a map?' said Gretel.

'There's no map,' I said. 'Whoever dug it up and reburied it didn't want it to be rediscovered. And Principal Greenbeard is pretty old. It must have been buried for at least seventy years . . . maybe even longer!'

The ground was hard. I kicked it with the toe of my shoe. It hurt.

'Ouch!' I said.

'So close and yet so far,' sighed Jenny.

'No wonder they couldn't find it again,' said Jack. 'It's hopeless.'

'Don't give up,' I said. 'Remember what Mr Brainfright said? We can make history . . . but not if we give up.'

'Perhaps "giving up" is the history we're going to make,' said Jack. 'Did you think of that?'

'No,' I said, 'because I'm not going to give up.'

'Then how are you going to find it?' said Jack.

'We need to think like pirates,' I said. 'Put ourselves in their shoes.'

'If we were pirates, wouldn't we be wearing boots?' said Newton.

'Yeah, good point, Newton,' said Jenny.

'Thanks, Jenny,' said Newton, beaming at her.

'All right, all right,' I said. 'Suppose you were a pirate and you were standing here in your *boots*, and you had a whole heap of treasure. Where would you bury it?'

'I wouldn't bury it in the first place,' said Gretel. 'I'd spend it.'

'But what if you couldn't spend it?' I said.

'I'd bury it,' said Gretel.

'Okay,' I said. 'Now we're really getting somewhere. Where would you bury it?'

'In my backyard,' she said.

'But you're a pirate!' I said. 'You don't have a backyard! You live on a ship.'

'Then I don't want to be a pirate,' said Gretel. 'I love my backyard. And I hate ships.'

I shook my head.

This wasn't getting us any closer to finding the treasure. I thought about the note. *Dig for one thousand nights and a night . . . for one thousand nights and a night . . . one thousand nights and a night . . .* There was something about that expression that seemed very familiar, but I couldn't place it.

'Are you okay, Henry?' said Jenny.

'Yes, I'm fine,' I said. 'I was just thinking about the note. It said "one thousand nights and a night". What does that mean to you?'

'A really long time,' said Jack.

'Right,' I said. 'But it's a funny way to say it, don't you think?'

'I guess so,' said Jenny. 'But it rhymes.'

And then it hit me. 'It's also the name of a very

famous book,' I said. *'The Book of the Thousand and One Nights!'*

'So?' said Jack.

'So we need a copy of that book!'

24
Mr Shush

Fortunately, the lesson after lunch was Library. Unfortunately, before we could go in we had to listen to Mr Shush's regular lecture.

Mr Shush was the school librarian.

Mr Shush loved his library.

Mr Shush loved books.

Mr Shush loved silence.

Mr Shush did *not* love students coming into his library and messing up all the books and breaking the silence with their noise.

We knew this because he told us so at the start of every library lesson. And today was no exception.

'You are here to find a book and read it,' he said as we stood in a line outside the library. 'You are not here to whisper. You are not here to talk. You are not here to laugh. You are not here to shout. You are not here to lean back on the chairs,

84

draw pictures or stare out of the window. Is that understood?'

'Yes, Mr Shush,' we all said.

But Mr Shush hadn't finished yet.

'You are here to READ books,' he continued. 'You are not here to flick through books. You are not here to FOLD the corners of their pages. You are not here to DROP books, THROW books or WRITE in books. Is that clear?'

'Yes, Mr Shush,' we all said.

'And if you borrow a book,' he said, 'you are to look after that book! You are to keep it in your book bag at all times—'

'Even when we're reading it?' said Jack.

'*Except* for when you are reading it, you silly boy,' said Mr Shush, rolling his eyes. 'You are not to eat or drink while reading a library book. You are not to take a library book to the beach and get sand in its spine. You are not to leave a library book at the bottom of your locker with old pieces of fruit and mouldy sandwiches. Do I make myself clear?'

'Yes,' we said, our heads spinning with the heavy responsibilities that came with being users of Mr Shush's library.

'All right then,' he said reluctantly. 'You may enter.'

We all walked slowly into the library, placed

our reading folders quietly down on the tables, and then proceeded to break pretty much every rule that we'd just been reminded about, sending poor Mr Shush into a shushing frenzy.

I found a copy of *The Book of the Thousand and One Nights*. I scanned the table of contents: there were stories about fishermen and princes and barbers and birds and beasts and gold, but nothing about pirates or buried treasure.

'Well,' said Jack, 'does it tell us where the treasure is?'

'No,' I said. 'Sorry. False alarm.'

'Can I have a look, Henry?' said Jenny.

'Sure,' I said, sliding the book across the table to her.

'DON'T SLIDE BOOKS ACROSS THE TABLE!' said Mr Shush, who was suddenly right behind me. 'How many times have I told you, if you *must* pass a book, then pass it by hand.'

'Sorry, Mr Shush,' I said.

Jack tried to stifle a laugh.

'Shush, Jack!' bellowed Mr Shush. 'People are trying to read.'

Jack nodded and Mr Shush moved on to find somebody else to yell at.

'Now, this is interesting,' said Jenny.

'What is?' I asked.

Jenny tapped the open book. 'There's a story

here called "The Ruined Man Who Became Rich Again Through a Dream".'

'Yes,' said Jack, 'and your point is?'

'Think about the note,' said Jenny. *'But of your riches you will only* dream! It's a clue! A definite clue!'

'What's the story about?' I said.

'I don't know yet,' said Jenny, running her finger rapidly across the page. 'Let me see . . . It says that there was a ruined man who lived in Baghdad and one night he dreamed that a man told him to go to Cairo to seek his fortune.'

'And did he go?' said Newton.

'Yes,' said Jenny, nodding. 'But when he got there he was wrongly accused of being a thief and was thrown in jail.'

'Well, that's a great help!' said Jack.

'That's not the end of the story,' said Jenny. 'The police chief asked the man why he'd come to Cairo and so the man told him about the dream. The police chief laughed and said he'd had a similar dream in which a man told him to go to Baghdad where there was a white house with a courtyard and a fountain under which a treasure was buried. But the police chief said he was too smart to take any notice of dreams and he advised the man to do the same. The other man, though, realised that the house in the police chief's dream was his *own* house, so when he got out of jail he went straight home, dug under the fountain and found a huge bag of money!'

'Good for him,' said Jack. 'But I don't see how that helps us.'

'I do,' I said. 'The man went all the way to Cairo looking for the treasure but the treasure was right in the place where he started. He never thought to look for it in his own backyard.'

'Do you think it's possible that whoever dug the treasure up from Skull Island reburied it in the same place?' said Jenny.

'I reckon so,' I said. 'What better place to hide a treasure from someone than in the very place that person has already looked? It's the one place they could count on Greenbeard and his gang *not* looking!'

'But that's so devious,' said Jenny.

'We are talking about pirates,' I said.

'*Pretend* pirates,' said Jack.

'Pirates nevertheless,' I said, firmly.

'If you're right, and it really is buried on Skull Island, then that narrows it down a lot,' said Gretel. 'But there's still an awful lot of Skull Island to search. It could take months to dig it all up.'

'Perhaps,' I said. 'But perhaps not if we think like pirates.'

'If I was a pirate,' said Newton, 'I'd get a metal detector.'

'Pirates don't have metal detectors,' I said.

'Maybe not,' said Newton. 'But I bet Grant Gadget does.'

'You're a genius, Newton!' I said.

'Do you think so?' said Newton, looking terrified.

'No doubt about it,' I said.

'Does that mean I'll have to leave Northwest Southeast Central School and go to Northwest Southeast Central School for the Gifted? But I don't want to leave! I like it here! I'll be lonely! I'll—'

'Calm down, Newton,' I said. 'I didn't mean you're *actually* a genius. It's just an expression—'

'So what are you saying?' said Newton, looking even more alarmed. 'That I'm stupid? That I'm going to have to go to Northwest Southeast Central School for the Non-gifted?'

'Don't worry about it, Newton,' I said. 'You're already at it! All I'm saying is that asking Grant Gadget for help is a good idea.'

'Oh,' said Newton. 'Thanks.'

'I'm not sure it is such a good idea,' said Jack. 'I've never seen one of Grant's dad's inventions actually work.'

'It's worth a try, though,' said Jenny. 'A metal detector that doesn't actually work is better than not having a metal detector at all.'

'I'm not so sure about that either,' said Jack.

25
Grant Gadget

'So,' said Jenny, 'are you going to ask Grant about the metal detector?'

'Shush!' said Mr Shush, coming up behind us.

'Sorry, Mr Shush,' said Jenny.

'Don't say sorry,' said Mr Shush, 'just be quiet!'

Jenny nodded. 'Okay, sorry,' she whispered.

Mr Shush rolled his eyes and then moved on to the next problem threatening the peace of his library: Clive was pushing the books on one side of the shelf so that the books on the other side were falling off onto Fiona's feet.

Typical Clive. The only thing he could think of to do with books was use them to hurt or annoy other people.

'Well?' said Jenny, as Mr Shush got busy with Clive. 'Are you going to ask him?'

'Yes,' I said. 'I'm just waiting until Mr Shush is distracted.'

'He's distracted now,' said Jenny, nodding towards Mr Shush, who was making Clive pick up all the books he'd pushed off the shelf.

'Okay, okay,' I said. 'I'm going!'

I got up and walked over to Grant.

He was deeply involved in a book on robots. In fact, he was so deeply involved he didn't even hear me say his name.

I tapped him on the shoulder. 'Grant!' I repeated.

He looked up, turned his head slowly, and blinked at me through his glasses. 'What is it, Henry?' he said.

'I wanted to ask you a favour,' I said.

'What?'

'I was wondering if you had a metal detector that you could lend me?'

Grant's eyebrows rose. 'What for?' he said.

'Oh, nothing,' I said, 'just some, you know, metal detecting.'

Grant frowned. 'You need to be more specific,' he said. 'What sort of metal?'

'I thought there was only one sort of metal,' I said.

Grant shook his head as if he were an adult and I was a poor misguided child. 'Oh, no,' he said. 'Metal comes in many different forms. Gold, silver, bronze, brass, platinum—'

'I get the idea, Grant,' I said, glancing over at the magazine area where Mr Shush was dealing with Penny and Gina who, as far as I could tell, had knocked over a magazine rack while they'd been prancing about on their imaginary horses. It wasn't going to occupy him forever, though. 'I want a detector that can detect all of them. Especially treasure.'

'Treasure?' said Grant. 'What sort of treasure?'

I hesitated, not sure how much to tell him. But I was running out of time.

'Buried treasure,' I said.

Grant nodded knowingly. 'I see,' he said. 'Well, that changes everything.'

'It does?' I said.

'Yes,' said Grant. 'It just so happens that my dad has been working on a buried-treasure detector. I don't want to bore or confuse you with the technical details, but it's basically a super-charged metal detector that can detect treasure no matter how deep it's buried.'

'Wow!' I said. 'That's exactly what we need!'

'We?' said Grant.

'I mean I,' I said.

'You said *we*,' said Grant. 'Who else is involved?'

'Just me and Jenny and Jack and Newton and Gretel,' I said.

'I see,' said Grant.

'Will you help us?'

'I can,' said Grant, 'but at a price.'

'What price?' I said.

'An equal share of the treasure.'

'No way,' I said.

'Forget it then,' said Grant.

I suddenly had second thoughts. I wanted that treasure.

'Way,' I said.

'Deal,' said Grant. 'I'll, er, borrow it from my dad's workshop tonight. Where's the treasure?'

'Promise you won't tell anyone?'

'I promise.'

'Cross your heart, hope to die, stick a needle in your eye?'

'Are you kidding?' said Grant. 'The eye is one of the most complex and delicate sense organs of the body. I'm certainly not going to stick a needle in it!'

'All right,' I said. 'But you won't tell anybody?'

'Of course not,' said Grant.

'It's buried in the school grounds,' I said.

'That's a very large area,' Grant said. 'Can you be any more specific?'

'I'll be more specific tomorrow, when you show me the buried-treasure detector.'

'Okay. Meet me at my locker at lunchtime tomorrow and we'll go treasure hunting.'

'Thanks, Grant,' I said.

I stood up, turned around, and looked straight into the eyes of Mr Shush.

'Shush!' he said.

26
The buried-treasure detector

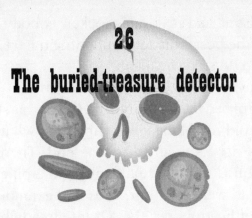

At exactly 12.04 the next day, we turned up at Grant's locker.

It was easy to tell Grant's locker. It had a large red sticker on the front that warned: TOP SECRET!

Grant was waiting for us. He looked at his watch. 'Thirty-five seconds late,' he said. 'What kept you?'

'Have you got the metal detector?' Jack asked.

'Not just a metal detector,' said Grant. 'A super-charged treasure detector! Turn around and I'll get it out—and no trying to peek inside my locker, or the deal is off.'

Nobody had ever seen inside Grant's locker . . . though not for lack of trying.

'No peeking,' said Jenny. 'Come on, you heard Grant, everybody turn around.'

We turned around and closed our eyes.

As much as we would have loved to see what

stuff Grant had inside his locker, nobody wanted to risk the possibility of not finding the treasure in order to do so.

'Okay, you can look now,' said Grant.

We turned back around and Grant was standing there holding a long silver pipe with what looked like a Frisbee attached to one end. There was a control box mounted halfway up the pipe. At the other end were two thin wires that extended up to a pair of headphones that Grant already had over his ears.

'What's that supposed to be?' said Jack.

'It's the buried-treasure detector, of course,' said Grant, talking very loudly. 'We're going to use it to find the buried treasure, remember?'

'Quiet!' I said, looking around to make sure nobody else had heard. 'Not so loud, Grant!'

'What?' he asked.

I lifted up one of his headphones. 'Don't shout!'

'Sorry,' he said. 'It's the headphones. I can't tell that I'm speaking loudly.'

He removed them and looped them around his neck. 'Well, what do you think? Isn't she a beauty?'

'No offence, but it looks like a pole with a Frisbee on the end,' said Jack.

'That shows how much you know!' Grant huffed.

'I think it looks amazing!' said Jenny quickly, before Jack could respond. 'Your dad must be so smart!'

'I helped him, of course,' said Grant. 'But yes, he *is* a brilliant inventor. So are you going to show me where this treasure is or not?'

'I thought you were going to show us,' said Jack.

'Jack,' I said, 'give him a break.'

'I probably could find it without your help,' said Grant, 'but it might take a little longer. And besides, a deal's a deal. I get a one-sixth share, right?'

We all looked at one another and nodded.

'Right,' I said. 'Come with us.'

We walked up to the top of Skull Island.

'It's buried somewhere on this hill,' I said, 'but we don't know exactly where.'

Grant nodded. 'Don't worry,' he told us, patting the buried-treasure detector and putting the headphones back on. 'That's where this comes in. Stand back. I'm going to turn it on. This thing is pretty powerful.'

'What's going to happen?' asked Newton nervously, backing away.

'What?' said Grant. 'I can't hear you! I've got headphones on.'

Grant pressed a button.

We heard a loud squeal from the headphones.

Grant tore them off his head.

'What is it?' said Jack. 'Have you found the treasure? Or are you picking up signals from outer space?'

'No,' said Grant. 'The volume was up too loud. It's the first time it's been used. It needs a little adjustment.'

'A lot of adjustment, I'd say,' said Jack.

Grant ignored him. He tweaked a dial and put the headphones back on.

This time there was no squeal.

Grant began walking in slow circles around the top of the hill. He had a look of intense concentration on his face.

'It's working!' said Jenny.

'How do you know it's working?' said Jack. 'He hasn't found the treasure yet.'

Suddenly Grant's buried-treasure detector started to vibrate.

The Frisbee clamped itself to the ground.

Grant pulled the headphones off. 'It's down there,' he said. He flashed a 'told you so' look at Jack.

'Grab a stick,' said Gretel, 'and let's start digging.'

We did as Gretel suggested, attacking the hard ground with sticks.

We gave it everything we had, but after five

minutes of frenzied digging there was still no sign of treasure.

'Are you sure it's here?' Jack asked.

'That's what the treasure detector indicated,' said Grant. 'And it's never been wrong.'

'It's never been right, either,' said Jack.

'You're just jealous,' said Grant.

'Hang on!' said Jenny. 'I've found something!'

We looked.

Her stick was definitely hitting a piece of metal. It didn't look like a chest full of buried treasure, but it definitely looked like metal.

She dug a little more and pulled out a small rusty disc.

'Is it a coin?' said Gretel.

'No, even better,' said Jenny. 'It's a smiley-face badge!'

'And that's it?' said Jack. 'That's the treasure?'

'My mum says a smile is priceless,' said Jenny, as she happily pinned the badge to the collar of her shirt.

'Yeah, but it's not treasure, is it?' Jack pointed out.

'No,' said Jenny. 'But I think it's a really good sign. Let's keep looking!'

Grant fired up his buried-treasure detector again. This time he got halfway down the hill before it started vibrating and squealing.

'There's something here,' he said. 'I can't say whether it's the treasure for sure, but it's definitely something.'

We got down and started digging again.

This time we found an old whistle on a chain.

'Probably belonged to Mr Grunt,' said Jack.

Mr Grunt is the sports teacher. He's very fond of blowing his whistle.

'Can I have it?' said Newton. 'I've always wanted a whistle. I can blow it if I get into trouble.'

'Sure,' I said, handing it to Newton.

Newton picked the dirt out of it and gave it a blow. It still worked. And it was LOUD. Pretty impressive for a whistle that had been buried for who knows how long. But as impressive as it was, it wasn't the treasure.

Grant started waving his buried-treasure detector over the ground again.

It only took a few minutes before it started shaking uncontrollably.

Suddenly Grant fell to his knees, then slumped sideways onto the ground.

Smoke began to pour from the control box. An amazing screaming noise came from the headphones.

Newton started blowing his whistle. 'Danger!' he yelled. 'Get back, everyone! Dangerous danger!'

I had to hand it to Newton. He sure knew what to do in a crisis.

Grant was still lying on the ground.

Then the buried-treasure detector blew up with a loud bang.

Grant sat up, dazed. He took off the headphones and rubbed his ears.

'Are you all right?' Jenny asked, kneeling beside him.

'Guess it needs a few adjustments,' he replied.

'A few?' said Jack. 'I think it's back to the drawing board on that one.'

Meanwhile Gretel was on her knees, digging furiously in the spot where Grant's buried-treasure detector had blown its top.

'Hey, look at this!' she said, holding up a small object. 'It's a key!'

We crowded around her.

'Can I have a look?' I said.

'Sure,' said Gretel, handing it to me.

I rubbed the dirt off the key and examined it closely. It had an engraving of a skull and crossbones on it.

'It's not the treasure,' I said, 'but it's the next best thing. We're definitely in the right spot.'

'Right spot for what?' said a voice over my shoulder.

I slipped the key into my pocket and turned around.

It was Fred Durkin, with Clive leering over his shoulder.

'Yeah, McThrottle,' said Clive. 'Right spot for what?'

'Testing out Grant's metal detector,' I said.

'Is that all you were doing?' Fred asked suspiciously.

'That's all,' I said.

Fred looked at me. 'If you're up to something, McThrottle, I'm going to find out what it is.'

Gretel stepped in. 'He's not up to anything,' she said. 'Run away and play now, boys.'

Fred just stared at her. 'Come on, Clive,' he said. 'This is getting boring.'

We watched them retreat down the hill.

'It was lucky for them they left when they did,' said Jack, punching his fist into his open palm. 'I was just about to teach those two thickheads a lesson they would never forget.'

'I thought you had sore fingers,' I said.

'Yeah, I did. But that was yesterday. They're better now.'

'Right,' I said, smiling. Jack was always so brave—once the danger had passed.

'What now?' Jenny asked, clearly relieved that the unfriendly encounter was over.

'We've got the key,' I said. 'And I'd say it's a fair bet the chest is not far away.'

At that moment the bell rang.

'Everyone meet back here tomorrow lunchtime, with shovels. And, remember, not a word to anybody!'

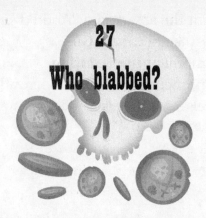

27
Who blabbed?

The next morning it was raining hard. As I walked into the classroom, Gina and Penny came running up to me.

'Henry,' said Gina, 'have you heard?'

'Heard what?' I asked.

'About the treasure!' Penny exclaimed.

I couldn't believe it. They knew already! But how? And how much did they know?

'What treasure?' I said, playing dumb.

'Well, there's a treasure worth millions and millions of dollars hidden somewhere under the school,' said Gina.

'Yeah!' said Penny. 'It was hidden there thousands of years ago by an evil pirate, and we're going to find it and buy a horse farm!'

'With riding trails!' said Gina.

Not with my treasure, you're not, I thought, but I tried not to look too annoyed. 'Who told you about the treasure?' I said.

'Well, it's a secret,' said Gina.

'I promise I won't tell anyone,' I said.

'Okay,' said Gina. 'It was Fiona.'

I went straight to Fiona's desk. She was deep in conversation with David. They were studying a book called *How to Find Buried Treasure*. When they realised I was standing there they both looked up. Fiona quickly shoved the book under her folder.

'Yes, Henry?' she said. 'What do you want?'

'What's with the book?' I asked.

'Nothing,' said Fiona.

'You wouldn't be thinking about looking for buried treasure, would you?' I said.

'Treasure?' Fiona shook her head a little too vigorously. 'I don't know what you're talking about.'

'Who told you?' I pressed.

'Told us what?' said David.

'About the treasure!'

Fiona and David looked at each other. They looked back at me.

'I know you know,' I said. 'And you know I know you know. So you might as well tell me who told you. It will save time.'

'Jenny told me,' said Fiona. 'But it's a secret, so don't tell anybody else.'

'Okay,' I said.

I went to Jenny's desk.

'Jenny,' I said, 'did you happen to tell anyone about the treasure?'

'No,' she said. 'I don't think so.'

'You don't *think* so?' I said.

'Hmmm,' said Jenny, thinking. 'Well, maybe I did tell one person. But just one. No more.'

'Would that person have been Fiona McBrain, by any chance?'

'Yes,' said Jenny.

'But why?' I said. 'You promised not to tell anybody else. You took an oath!'

'I know,' said Jenny, looking very apologetic. 'I'm sorry, Henry. It just kind of came out.'

'How does something like that "just kind of come out"?'

'Well, she asked me what we were doing on the hill with Grant and the metal detector and I couldn't tell her a lie. I can't lie to a friend, Henry! But I made her promise not to tell anybody else.'

'Well, she has,' I said. 'She told Gina and Penny, and they're telling EVERYBODY!'

'I'm so sorry, Henry,' said Jenny. 'You won't make me stick a needle in my eye, will you?'

'Not this time,' I said. 'But definitely next time!'

Jack came up to us.

'Everybody knows!' he said. 'Did Newton blab? I knew it. I knew we couldn't trust him. I knew it!'

'It wasn't Newton,' I told him.

'It was me,' said Jenny in a small voice.

'I knew it!' said Jack. 'I knew we couldn't trust a girl! I knew it!'

'I beg your pardon?' said Gretel, coming up behind Jack and putting a large hand on his shoulder. 'What's that you're saying about girls?'

Jack looked at Gretel's hand. 'Oh,' he said. 'Um . . . er . . . I was just saying I knew we could trust a girl to find the treasure. They're very good at finding things, girls . . . much better than boys.'

'Are you *sure* that's what you said?' said Gretel.

Jack nodded. 'I'm sure I'm sure,' he said. 'I'm even sure that I'm sure that I'm sure that I'm sure.'

'Okay,' said Gretel, taking her hand off his shoulder. 'That's fine then.'

The only thing that wasn't fine, of course, was that now everybody knew about the treasure!

28

A wonderful morning

At that moment, Mr Brainfright came into the classroom. He was soaking wet and whistling loudly. He took off his coat and shook it. The water made a big puddle on the floor. Then he hung it up.

'Good morning, class,' he said brightly. 'And what a wonderful morning it is!'

'Um,' said Fiona, 'I don't want to be rude, but it's actually not that wonderful. It's pouring rain, there's thunder and lightning, and it's freezing.'

'Perfect!' said Mr Brainfright. 'I couldn't ask for anything better!'

'Are you saying you *like* this weather?' Fiona clearly couldn't believe what she was hearing.

'I love it!' said Mr Brainfright.

'I hate it,' said Fiona. 'I love sunny weather.'

'I love that too!' said Mr Brainfright.

'How can you love sunny weather *and* rainy weather?' said Fiona.

'I love all weather,' said Mr Brainfright. 'It keeps life interesting.'

'Not when it's wet and cold, though,' said Fiona.

'But you're not wet right now, are you?' asked Mr Brainfright.

'No,' Fiona admitted.

'Are you cold right now?'

'No,' said Fiona. 'Kind of warm, actually.'

'So what you're telling me is that you're warm and dry,' said Mr Brainfright. 'What else is going right for you at this moment despite the fact that it's a cold wet day?'

Fiona shrugged.

'Who can help Fiona?' said Mr Brainfright. 'What are some other things she has to be happy about right now?'

'She has a chair to sit on?' Jenny said.

'Exactly!' said Mr Brainfright. 'The weather doesn't change that fact! What else does Fiona have to be grateful about, no matter what the weather is like?'

'She has a desk?' I said.

'Yes!' said Mr Brainfright. 'Keep them coming!'

'She's got a body!' said Grant.

'She's got a head!' said Gretel.

'She's got a brain!' said Newton.

'Yes,' said Mr Brainfright. 'And not just Fiona—you all have!'

'Clive hasn't,' said Jack.

'I'm going to tell my brother you said that,' said Clive.

'Wonderful!' said Mr Brainfright. 'Clive has a brother to whom he can tell everything! What else do you have to be grateful for?'

'Arm wrestling!' said Gretel.

'Ice-cream!' said Jack.

'Bandaids!' said Newton.

'Friends!' said Jenny.

'Excellent!' said Mr Brainfright, as the classroom lit up with a fresh flash of lightning, followed almost immediately by a peal of thunder which sounded like it was only a few metres above the roof. 'Now repeat those things with feeling. You are grateful for them. Yell them out as if that's really the case.'

'ARM WRESTLING!' yelled Gretel.

'ICE-CREAM!' yelled Jack.

'BANDAIDS!' yelled Newton.

'FRIENDS!' yelled Jenny.

'I still can't hear you!' said Mr Brainfright. 'Stand up on your desks and tell me again!'

'ARM WRESTLING!' yelled Gretel.

'ICE-CREAM!' yelled Jack.

'BANDAIDS!' yelled Newton.

'FRIENDS!' yelled Jenny.

Mr Brainfright was smiling broadly. 'That's better!' he said. 'Now, keep repeating those words while everybody else gets up on their desks and yells out one of their own favourite things!'

'Will we be tested on this?' asked Fiona.

'Yes,' said Mr Brainfright. 'The happier you feel, the better your mark.'

'But how will you know?' said Fiona.

'I won't,' said Mr Brainfright. 'But *you* will.'

'Huh?' said Fiona. 'What sort of test is that?'

'The most important sort!' said Mr Brainfright. 'But don't take my word for it. Try it out and see for yourself.'

Nobody needed any further encouragement.

Every single 5C student climbed onto their desk and began yelling out their favourite thing at the top of their voice.

'CHOCOLATE!'

'WEEKENDS!'

'MOVIES!'

'COMPUTERS!'

'PENGUINS!'

'PONIES!'

'MOTORBIKES!'

'GRANDMOTHERS!'

'PONIES!'

'POTATO CHIPS!'

111

'DINOSAURS!'

'MUSIC!'

'MUD!'

'PIRATES!'

'TREASURE!'

The students were making more noise than the storm that continued to rage outside. This fact didn't go unnoticed by Mrs Cross, who appeared at the door of the classroom, red-faced and puffing.

'I'm trying to teach algebra!' she yelled.

'Now that's one that nobody has mentioned so far,' said Mr Brainfright.

'ALGEBRA!' yelled Fiona.

Mrs Cross looked at Fiona. 'You used to be such a nice, quiet girl, Fiona,' she said. 'What happened?'

'ALGEBRA!' Fiona shouted again.

Mrs Cross shook her head and turned her attention back to Mr Brainfright. 'This is all your doing!' she scolded. 'This was a quiet, orderly school until you arrived.'

'Quiet and orderly does not necessarily mean that the students are learning anything,' countered Mr Brainfright.

'I can't see that they are learning anything standing on their desks and yelling at the top of their voices!' Mrs Cross cried. 'I may be old-fashioned, Mr Brainfright, but I believe learning happens *at* desks, not *on* them. I'll be reporting this to Principal Greenbeard. If you can't keep order, I'm sure that he can!'

Mrs Cross turned on her heels and marched towards the door.

'ALGEBRA!' shouted Fiona, triggering another enthusiastic round of shouting amongst the class.

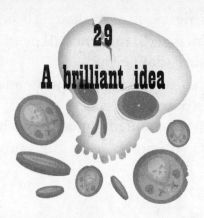

29
A brilliant idea

Fortunately, the sun came out at lunchtime.

Unfortunately, Skull Island was covered with fifth-grade treasure seekers all desperately digging with sticks, rulers, pens, pencils and even their bare hands.

Jenny, Gretel, Jack, Newton and I stood at the bottom and watched. Grant wasn't with us. He was too busy repairing his buried-treasure detector to look for real buried treasure.

'We have to stop them!' said Jack. 'They're trying to steal our treasure!'

Jenny was frantic.

'I'm so sorry, so sorry. I'm such an idiot. I've ruined everything,' she said. 'They're going to find it before we do—and it's all my fault!'

'Don't worry,' I said. 'We'll find it.'

'Find what?' said a voice behind me.

I turned around.

It was Fred.

'I don't know what you're talking about, Fred,' I said.

'I think you do,' he spat back.

'No, I don't!' I said.

'He does!' said Clive.

'He does not!' said Gretel.

'He does so!' said Clive. 'And so do you!'

'No they don't!' said Jack. 'They don't know anything. And neither do I. Or Newton. Or Jenny. None of us knows anything about anything. And of all the things we don't know anything about, we especially don't know anything about secret buried treasure!'

'Secret buried treasure, eh?' said Fred. 'If it's so secret, how do *you* know about it?'

Jack took a breath to reply but then stopped.

He didn't know what to say.

Fred had outsmarted him.

For a dumb guy, Fred could actually be pretty smart sometimes.

But not as smart as me.

I thought fast.

Faster than I've ever thought in my life.

Faster even than the speed of thought.

And then I had a brilliant idea . . .

The most brilliant idea I'd ever had. (At least for that morning, anyway.)

It was an idea that would not only get Fred off our back, but would also help clear Skull Island of all the unwanted treasure seekers.

I would tell Fred the truth. Well, sort of.

'All right, Fred,' I said. 'You win. You're obviously too clever for us. There *is* a treasure.'

'I knew it!' said Fred.

'I told you so!' said Clive.

'Henry!' said Jack.

'No, Jack,' I went on. 'No more lies. It's time for the truth. Principal Greenbeard buried a treasure many years ago when he was a student at Northwest Southeast Central School, and it's still here.'

'How do you know all this?' Fred asked.

'I found out about it when I got sent to his office the other day,' I told him.

Fred eyed me suspiciously. 'How do I know you're telling the truth?'

'I can prove it,' I said. 'I've got a map.'

'You've got a map?' said Gretel, dumbfounded.

'Yes,' I said. 'I swiped it from Principal Greenbeard's desk when he wasn't looking. It shows the exact location of the treasure.'

'Why didn't you tell *us* about it?' said Jack.

'Sorry,' I said, 'but I didn't want everybody to find out. I made up the stuff about it being on Skull Island to protect the real location. But it's no use: Fred's too clever for us.'

'Since when?' said Gretel, making a fist.

'Don't even think about it, One-punch,' said Fred. 'I want that map, McThrottle.'

'What will you give me for it?' I said.

'It's not so much what I *will* give you as what I *won't* give you. If you give me the map I won't give you a neck squeeze so hard that your head pops like a pimple.'

'I'd like to see you try,' said Gretel.

'I'd like to see you try to stop me,' said Fred.

'I'd like to see you try to stop me stopping you!' said Gretel.

Newton was getting ready to blow his whistle.

I put my hand over it to stop him. 'It's a deal,' I said.

'What?' said Jack. 'You double-crosser! Don't give him the map!'

'Easy for you to say,' I said. 'It's not your neck that's going to get squeezed or your head that's going to pop like a pimple.'

'But it could be very easily arranged,' said Fred.

'No, thanks,' said Jack, shaking his head and then turning to me. 'I thought we were friends, Henry. But I see I was wrong. I'm leaving.'

'Me too,' said Gretel, shaking her head in disgust. 'Are you coming, Newton?'

Newton just nodded sadly and followed Gretel and Jack down the hill.

Jenny could barely look at me. I'd never seen her look so hurt or shocked. 'A true friend would have told us about the map,' she said. Then she followed the others off the hill.

I shrugged.

'You're better off without those bozos,' said Fred. 'Now give me the map. I haven't got all day, you know.'

'I don't have it here,' I told him. 'It's at home. I'll bring it tomorrow.'

'Make sure you do, McThrottle,' Fred warned. 'First thing. Before school.'

'Yeah,' said Clive. 'Make sure . . . or else.'

Fred and Clive laughed and headed off towards the canteen.

I waited until they were out of sight and then went after the others.

I had some explaining to do.

30
Dirty double-double crosser

I found Gretel, Jack, Newton and Jenny in our favourite spot at the side of the basketball court.

'Why are you here?' said Jack. 'Don't your new friends want to play with you anymore?'

'They're not my friends,' I said. 'You are!'

'Well you sure don't act like it,' said Gretel. 'Real friends trust each other.'

'I *do* trust you,' I said.

'Why didn't you tell us about the map, then?' asked Jenny.

'Because there is no map,' I said.

'What do you mean?' Newton was perplexed. 'You just told Fred that you had one. If you don't give him a map, he's going to squeeze your neck so hard that your head will pop like a pimple.'

'I'll give him a map, all right,' I said. 'A *fake* map with the treasure marked as far away from Skull Island as possible. It will get Fred and Clive off our backs, and we'll let everybody else know about it as well. Skull Island will be all ours again.'

'Great idea, Henry!' said Jenny. 'I knew you weren't really a dirty double-crosser.'

'Well, actually I am,' I said. 'I'm going to double-cross Fred with the fake map.'

'Oh, yeah,' said Jenny, frowning.

'And then, to make it even more complicated, I'm going to double-double-cross Fred by telling him that I told you all that it's a fake map. Then we'll be able to continue digging on Skull Island where we know the treasure *really* is.'

'Wow,' said Jenny. 'You're a dirty double-*double*-crosser!'

'Very clever, Henry,' said Jack. 'But where are we going to get a fake treasure map?'

'We're going to make one, of course,' I said.

'And just how do we do that?' said Jack.

'Easy!' I said.

How to make a fake treasure map

1. Go to the art room.
2. Tell the art teacher, Mrs Rainbow, that you all love art so much that you can't wait for your weekly art lesson—you want to do it at lunchtime. She will be very happy to let you in. She loves enthusiastic students.
3. To make a fake treasure map you will need:
   Paper.
   Pens.
   Cold tea.
   A candle.
   A cottonwool ball.
   A piece of ribbon.
4. Ask Mrs Rainbow for all of these things.
5. Draw a map of the school. Get Jack to do it because he's the best drawer, and he can draw really good maps.
6. Draw a skull and crossbones in the top

right-hand corner of the paper.

7. Draw a compass in the top left-hand corner.

8. Write NORTH at the top of the map, SOUTH at the bottom, EAST on the right and WEST on the left.

9. Mark fake treasure location with an X.

10. Crumple up the paper.

11. Flatten it back out.

12. Crumple it up again.

13. Flatten it out again.

14. Crumple it up again.

15. Flatten it out again.

16. Argue with Jack about how many times you need to do this to give the map an authentically worn look.

17. Use cottonwool ball to dab cold tea on it. This will give your map an authentically old brown look.

18. Be careful not to accidentally use hot tea because it will burn your fingers when you dab your cottonwool ball into it. (Just ask Newton.)

19. If Newton does burn his fingers and causes the tea to spill all over the map, throw it away and repeat steps 5 to 17. Next time, don't let Newton anywhere near the tea.

20. Light the candle and carefully burn the edges of the paper. This will give your map that truly

authentic burnt-edged pirate map look. You will, of course, need Mrs Rainbow's help to do this because it's very easy to accidentally set fire to the map. (Just ask Newton.)

21. If Newton does set fire to your map, use what's left of the cold tea to put out the flames. Repeat steps 5 to 20, and don't let Newton anywhere near the candle.

22. Argue about why treasure maps have burnt edges. (Jenny thinks it's because pirates were very careless and always dropping their stuff in fires. When I pointed out that they lived on ships in the middle of the ocean, Jack suggested that the oceans were a lot more fiery in pirate days. But that's just stupid.)

23. Dry fake treasure map with a hair dryer.

24. Roll it up and tie it with a ribbon. This is how pirates always did things up because rubber bands hadn't been invented yet.

25. Hey, presto, you're done! You are now the proud owner of a real genuine authentic fake pirate-treasure map!

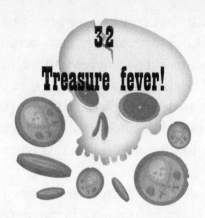

32
Treasure fever!

As I arrived at school the next morning it was obvious that word of the treasure had got around.

How did I know this?

Because I could see, even before I entered the gate, that pretty much everybody in the entire school was searching for it.

Anywhere there was a patch of grass or dirt, there were kids digging holes.

And where there wasn't any grass or dirt, kids were trying to dig holes in the asphalt. They weren't getting very far, but the thing was that they were trying.

There were kids digging on the front lawn area.

Kids digging on the sports field.

One boy was even digging in the flowerboxes outside Principal Greenbeard's office window.

Mr Spade was running around like a lunatic, chasing kids off the sports field and out of the flowerbeds. But he was fighting a losing battle. As soon as he chased one group of kids away, another group would start somewhere else.

The whole school had caught treasure fever!

The whole school had gone treasure mad!

Unfortunately, I wasn't about to help the situation. In fact, for my plan to work, I had to make it a whole lot worse. The first step was to give the map to Fred Durkin. The second step was to make sure that everybody *knew* Fred had a map.

The first step was pretty easy because Fred and Clive were waiting for me at the school gate.

'Well, if it isn't my old mate Henry McThrottle,' said Fred, smiling. 'Have you got my treasure map?'

'Of course,' I said, handing it over. 'Happy hunting.'

Fred and Clive pulled the ribbon off the map, unrolled it, and studied it quickly.

'What does the X mean?' Clive asked.

'It's where the treasure is, stupid!' Fred replied.

'What, right in the middle of the little kids' sandpit?'

'Well, that's where the X is.' Fred frowned. 'But something doesn't add up . . .'

'What could be more clear?' I said.

'If you knew this,' said Fred, 'then why were you digging on the hill?'

'I would have thought it was obvious,' I told him. 'I was double-crossing the others. I didn't want them to know where the treasure was *really* buried. I was going to do my own secret dig in the sandpit after school.'

Fred nodded with approval. 'Smart, McThrottle. Real smart. But you'd better not let me catch you digging in the sandpit or you'll regret it.'

'Don't worry,' I said. 'I know better than to try and double-cross someone as smart as you. And if you like, I'll keep digging on the hill to make sure the others don't give you any trouble.'

'But won't they get suspicious?' said Fred. 'They'll know that you gave me the map and I'll be digging in the sandpit.'

'I'll tell them I gave you a *fake* treasure map!' I said.

Fred smiled. 'Good work, McThrottle. You're pretty smart for a moron.'

'Thanks,' I said, my head spinning.

Double-crossing people sure was complicated.

But I wasn't finished yet.

33
Regaining Skull Island

After leaving Fred I made sure that as many people in the school as possible knew that:

1. Fred Durkin had the treasure map that indicated the true position of the treasure.

2. The treasure was buried in the junior sandpit.

To make sure that as many people in the school as possible knew, I told Gina and Penny. If you've got a secret that you want not to stay secret, telling Gina and Penny is the best way to make sure everybody knows about it. They cover a lot of ground on their imaginary horses.

Sure enough, word spread fast.

By lunchtime, Skull Island was all ours again.

We went straight to the spot where we found the key.

'Well done, Henry!' said Jack. 'We're the only ones here!'

'Everybody else is over at the junior sandpit,' said Jenny, who was standing on top of the hill. 'It looks kind of crowded.'

'I don't think Fred is going to be very happy about that,' said Newton.

'Fred is never very happy about anything,' Gretel pointed out. 'Even if he found the treasure, I don't think he'd be very happy.'

'Yeah, well,' said Jack, 'he's about as likely to find treasure in that sandpit as he is to find a brain in his brother's head.'

We all laughed.

'Come on,' said Gretel. 'We're wasting time. Let's dig!'

We'd all brought spades from home. That fact, plus the fact that the ground was softer after the rain, made digging a lot easier than it had been before.

Within fifteen minutes we had a very deep and impressive hole.

But no treasure.

'Where is it?' said Gretel. 'We found the key here. The treasure must be close by.'

'Maybe it's shifted over time,' said Jenny.

'How could that happen?' said Jack. 'You dig a hole. You put the treasure in. You put the dirt back in. The treasure doesn't go anywhere.'

'There might have been an earthquake,' said Jenny.

'An earthquake?' said Newton, looking scared.

'Don't worry, Newton,' said Jack. 'There are no earthquakes in Northwest Southeast Central. No earthquakes. No tornadoes. No floods. No fires. Northwest Southeast Central is the most boring place in the world.'

'I like it,' I said. 'Believe it or not, Jack, I don't want to get shaken up in an earthquake, sucked up by a tornado, washed away in a flood or burned up in a fire.'

'Henry,' said Jenny, 'you're scaring Newton.'

'Sorry,' I said, patting Newton on the shoulder. 'Don't worry, you're safe here.'

'Apart from the risk of falling into a big hole,' Jack added.

'Yikes!' said Newton.

'Well, I'm glad we got that settled,' said Gretel. 'Meanwhile, do we keep digging?'

'Definitely not!' said a familiar voice. Mrs Cross was walking up the hill towards us. 'I don't know what you kids think you're doing, digging a hole as big and as dangerous as that, but I want you to fill it in immediately and then go back to class!'

'But lunchtime hasn't finished yet,' said Jack.

Mrs Cross stared at Jack. 'It will be by the time you've finished filling in that hole,' she said.

'But everybody else is digging holes,' said Gretel.

'Just because everybody else is doing something doesn't make it right,' Mrs Cross chided. 'Fill in the hole before somebody falls in and hurts themselves or I'll send the lot of you to Principal Greenbeard's office.'

We started filling the hole in as Mrs Cross stomped back down the hill.

'Why is she picking on us?' asked Newton.

It was a good question.

I didn't know the answer then, though I do now.

At that moment, as we all got down on our hands and knees to fill in the hole, all I knew was that treasure hunting was turning out to be a lot of hard work . . . and not much fun.

34
How to make friends with a banana

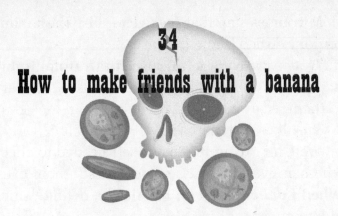

By the time the bell rang for the end of lunch we were exhausted.

And hungry.

Fortunately, when we came back into class there was a banana on each of our desks.

'Excuse me, Mr Brainfright,' said Fiona. 'There's a banana on my desk.'

'Ah, you've noticed!' Mr Brainfright looked pleased. 'Excellent observation, Fiona.'

'There's one on my desk, too!' said David.

'And mine!' said everybody else at the same time.

Mr Brainfright nodded. 'Very good,' he said. 'Nothing wrong with Class 5C's eyesight. But if you didn't have eyesight, how might you tell that there was a banana on your desk?'

'By smelling it?' said Jenny.

'Yes!' said Mr Brainfright. 'Now, everybody

close your eyes and see if you can *smell* the banana on your desk.'

By now we were getting used to Mr Brainfright's unusual lessons. In fact, we were looking forward to them.

We all closed our eyes.

Well, all except me, because I needed to check whether everybody else had closed their eyes. When I *did* close them, I noticed a definite smell of banana in the air.

'Well?' said Mr Brainfright. 'Who can smell their banana?'

'I can smell banana,' said Fiona, 'but I don't know if it's my banana or because the room is *full* of bananas.'

'You should be able to smell your own banana,' said Mr Brainfright. 'Every banana has its own unique smell. Its own unmistakable scent. No two bananas are alike.'

'Yes, they are,' said David, holding up his and Fiona's bananas. 'Look, they're both yellow, they're both curved, and they both smell like bananas!'

'At first glance, yes,' said Mr Brainfright. 'But take a closer look.' He took the bananas from David and held them up. 'Examine their markings. This one has a small black mark in the middle, whereas this other one has a slightly ragged black hat.'

It was funny, but as Mr Brainfright pointed out

the unique markings and features of the bananas, they began to seem as different from each other as, well, two bananas, I guess.

'All right,' said Mr Brainfright, 'now it's your turn. I want you to look at your banana. Not just look at it, but *really* look at it. Study your banana. Examine your banana. Give your banana a name.'

'A name?' said Jenny. 'For a banana?'

'Yes,' said Mr Brainfright. 'Why not? Make friends with your banana! Bananas are people too.'

'No, they're not,' said David. 'They're bananas!'

'Perhaps it might help if you draw a little face on it,' said Mr Brainfright. 'Like this.'

Mr Brainfright picked up a black marker and drew a happy little smiley face on his banana.

'There!' he said. 'How's that?'

David frowned.

The rest of the class laughed . . . and immediately began drawing faces on their bananas.

'I'm going to give my banana a name,' said Clive in a loud voice. 'I'm going to call mine Henry. And then I'm going to MASH it.'

I ignored Clive, but Jack couldn't. 'I'm going to call mine Fred,' he said, 'because it's got about as many brains as him.'

'I'm going to tell my brother you said that,' said Clive, 'and I can tell you now—'

133

'Yeah, I know, I know,' said Jack, 'he's not going to like it.'

'I'm going to tell him you finished my sentence, too!'

'I don't even care,' said Jack, 'because if your brother tries anything it's not just me he's going to have to deal with . . . it's my banana as well.'

Jack held up his banana. He'd drawn a really mean face on it. That was one scary banana. Definitely not the sort of banana you'd want to meet late at night in some dark alley.

'Don't fight, boys,' said Jenny, holding up her banana, which had a smiley face on it, almost identical to the smiley face on the badge she had found on Skull Island. 'Let's all be friends! Let's have a banana party!'

'I don't think so,' said Clive. 'You and your bananas are all freaks!'

'Oh, you hurt my banana's feelings!' said Jenny.

Which I'm pretty sure is what Clive was intending, but before he could reply, Mr Brainfright called us all to attention.

'Okay, class,' he said. 'Now you've all got to know your bananas a little better. You've studied them, smelled them, learned their names, given them faces and I note that some of you are even talking to your bananas and that your bananas are talking back to you. But now it's time to get to know them even better. It's time to eat your bananas.'

'EAT my banana?' said Jenny. 'But I could never do that. I LOVE my banana!'

'Never get emotionally attached to a piece of fruit,' said Mr Brainfright, in a gravely serious voice. 'You never know when you might have to eat it.'

35
Mr Brainfright's important lesson no. 3

Never get emotionally attached to a piece of fruit.
You never know when you might have to eat it.

36
How to eat a banana

'We are now going to learn how to eat a banana,' said Mr Brainfright.

'But we already know how to eat a banana,' said David.

'Oh, I'm sure you know how to shove a banana into your mouth while you're busy doing something else,' said Mr Brainfright. 'But I'm going to teach you how to eat a banana using all your senses.'

'Will we be tested on this?' asked Fiona.

'Yes,' said Mr Brainfright. 'If you can eat a banana feeling as much excitement as you'd feel going on a rollercoaster, you'll pass the test.'

'Huh?' said Fiona.

'True happiness in life comes from being able to appreciate the ordinary,' said Mr Brainfright, 'not just the extraordinary. Now, take your banana, pinch the top, and then peel one side down.'

Jenny had tears in her eyes. 'I can't do it!' she said. 'I can't!'

'It's okay,' I whispered to her. 'It *wants* you to.'

'It does?'

'Yes,' I said. 'It's your friend, right? And friends look after each other. Your banana is looking after you by giving you fresh vitamins and minerals and filling you up with bananary goodness.'

Yeah, I know, I sounded like an advertisement for breakfast cereal. But I didn't like to see Jenny upset. And it worked.

'Do you really think so, Henry?' she said.

'Yes,' I told her.

'Okay,' she said to her banana, pinching the top of its head. 'This won't hurt a bit, I promise. Well, it *will* hurt a bit, but not *too* much.'

'As you peel your banana,' said Mr Brainfright, 'don't forget to look at it. Smell it. Feel it. Listen to the sound of the peel as it splits. Then, and only then, when you've removed all the peel, *taste* your banana!'

I did as Mr Brainfright suggested.

I looked at it.

I smelled it.

I felt it.

I listened to it.

I tasted it.

Mr Brainfright was right. That banana tasted better than any other banana I've ever eaten in my whole life.

37

What to do with a banana peel

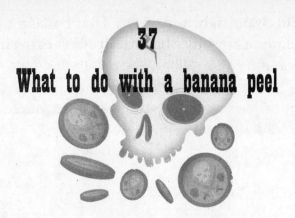

'Do we put the peel in the bin?' Jack asked after he'd finished his banana.

'Oh no!' said Mr Brainfright. 'The peel is the very best part!'

'We don't have to eat it, do we?' said Jack, looking as alarmed as Newton.

'No,' said Mr Brainfright, 'we can do something much more fun with it. Let me demonstrate.'

Mr Brainfright placed his banana peel carefully on the floor in front of his desk, yellow side up, and went to the door. Then, without warning, he ran and jumped on his banana peel, skidding about three metres before losing his balance and falling against the blackboard with a whoop of joy.

Just when we thought we'd seen everything, we saw something new.

We saw a teacher skidding on a banana peel.

And not by accident, either.

This was deliberate.

'Hang on,' said Mr Brainfright, 'that wasn't a very good one. What if I put the banana peel closer to the door and then took a run-up from the corridor? That would give me a longer ride.'

'Should I measure it?' asked Fiona.

'Great idea,' said Mr Brainfright. 'Let's do this properly.'

Mr Brainfright repositioned the banana, went out into the corridor, and bent down in a crouch.

'Count me down, Class 5C!' he said.

We were only too happy to oblige.

'TEN!' we yelled. 'NINE! EIGHT! SEVEN! SIX! FIVE! FOUR! THREE! TWO! ONE!'

Mr Brainfright took off explosively. He burst through the door and jumped onto the banana peel and sailed right across the room, this time without falling over.

He punched the air.

We cheered.

'Three and a half metres!' announced Fiona, tape measure in her hand.

'That's more like it!' said Mr Brainfright. 'Who thinks they can beat that?'

Of course we all put up our hands.

The next ten minutes was the most fun any of us have *ever* had in a classroom. We threw down our banana peels and started skidding.

We experimented with placing the banana peel right side up compared to upside down. Long run-ups versus short run-ups. Yelling as you ran compared to quiet runs.

There were a lot of collisions, sure, but we learned more about skidding on banana peels in that ten minutes than most of us had learned in the last ten years.

The skidding only lasted ten minutes due to the fact that Mrs Cross appeared in the middle of it all.

She was cross.

As cross as I've ever seen her.

Maybe even crosser.

If that was possible.

But not as cross as she was about to get.

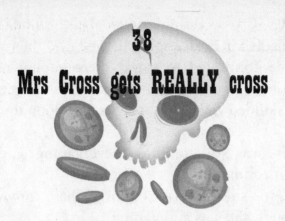

38
Mrs Cross gets REALLY cross

'WHAT DO YOU THINK YOU'RE DOING?' she yelled.

'Skidding on banana peels!' said David.

'Do you want to have a turn?' asked Fiona. 'You can borrow mine if you like. I'm not actually skidding. I'm recording the results. I'm going to make a graph.'

'Where's your teacher?' Mrs Cross demanded.

'Outside on the steps,' said David. 'He wanted to get a really good run-up to break his own skidding record.'

'What are you talking about, you silly boy?' said Mrs Cross.

At that moment we heard the sound of heavy footsteps.

'Here he comes!' said David. 'You'd better move out of the way! I'll explain later.'

But it was too late.

Mrs Cross, dumbfounded, just stood there gaping as Mr Brainfright charged into the room.

She continued to stand there gaping as Mr Brainfright launched himself onto his banana peel and skidded heroically across the floor towards her.

She was still standing there gaping when he slammed into her.

Then she wasn't standing there anymore, although she was still gaping.

She was also flying through the air.

Flying through the air—and then flying out the window!

39

Mrs Cross gets even crosser, maybe even the crossest she's ever been

Mr Brainfright crashed heavily into his desk and then fell down.

'Ooof!' he said as he lay there sprawled on the floor. 'Somebody please tell me that I didn't just bump into Mrs Cross and knock her out the window.'

The class was silent.

'Oh dear,' said Mr Brainfright, getting up and rubbing his head. 'So I *did* just bump into Mrs Cross and knock her out the window.'

We nodded.

Mr Brainfright went to the window.

We all followed him.

Poor Mrs Cross. I knew just how she felt.

She was lying on her back in Mr Spade's freshly dug flowerbed, looking up at us.

'I suppose you all think this is funny!' she shouted.

'No, of course not, Mrs Cross,' Mr Brainfright called down. 'Are you all right?'

'Yes,' said Mrs Cross, picking herself up out of the dirt, 'but *you're* not going to be by the time I get through with you!'

'Please don't hurt me, Mrs Cross,' said Mr Brainfright. 'It was an accident! It could have happened to anybody.'

'I'm not going to hurt you, Brainfright,' said Mrs Cross. 'But I *am* going to report you to Principal Greenbeard. I'll see to it that you never work in this school ever again!'

And with that, Mrs Cross stormed off across the playground towards Principal Greenbeard's office.

Mr Brainfright came away from the window and shook his head. 'Work?' he said. 'What's she talking about? I've never "worked" a day in my life. Especially not with this class. This is what I call fun!'

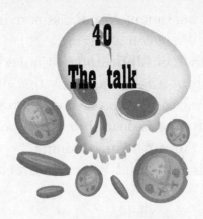

40
The talk

After we'd picked up all the banana peels and put all the desks and chairs back into order, we took our seats.

'What do you think is going to happen to Mr Brainfright?' Jenny whispered to me.

'Nothing will happen,' I whispered back. 'Mrs Cross will blow off a bit of steam in Principal Greenbeard's office, cool down, go back to her class, and everything will go on as usual. It's not the first time she's been cross with Mr Brainfright, you know.'

'I hope you're right, Henry.'

Mr Brainfright was in the middle of drawing a large banana on the blackboard when there was a knock on the door.

It was Principal Greenbeard. He saluted Mr Brainfright. 'Sorry to interrupt you in mid flow, but I wonder if you wouldn't mind dropping anchor for a moment and accompanying me into the gangway?'

'Certainly,' said Mr Brainfright, quickly finishing his drawing of a banana. 'Copy this picture into your workbooks, please, 5C. And then I want you to write fifty words describing what your banana tasted like. I'll be back in a minute.'

Mr Brainfright and Principal Greenbeard left the room.

The class was silent.

I could see Mr Brainfright's and Principal Greenbeard's heads as they stood and talked in the corridor, but despite how quiet everyone was I couldn't quite make out what they were saying.

Every now and then, though, Principal Greenbeard would raise his voice and I caught a few words, like 'not acceptable', 'shape up or ship out', 'review your position' and 'stay on course and stick to the program . . . or else.'

Mr Brainfright came back into the room.

'Close your workbooks,' he said quietly.

'But I haven't finished drawing my banana,' said Fiona.

'Or me,' said David.

'Never mind that now,' said Mr Brainfright. 'Apparently it is very important that we stick to the program. Can anybody tell me what you would normally be doing at this time of the week?'

'A spelling test,' said Fiona.

The rest of the class groaned.

Mr Brainfright sighed. 'A spelling test,' he mumbled to himself, shaking his head. 'Of all the amazing things we could be doing . . . but . . . no . . . must stick to the program. Very well, a spelling test is what we shall have.'

'Will we be tested on that?' asked Fiona.

'Yes,' said Mr Brainfright. 'I'm no expert, but I believe that's the general idea of a spelling test.'

'Here's the book,' said Fiona, handing him her copy of *Spelling is Fun*. 'We're up to test number twenty-two.'

'Spelling is fun,' said Mr Brainfright, reading the title aloud and then repeating it as if he was trying to convince himself of its truth. 'Spelling *is* fun. *Spelling* is fun. Spelling is *fun*!'

It was sad to see Mr Brainfright like this.

One minute he was teaching us how to skid on a banana peel, the next he was conducting a spelling test.

I glanced at Jenny. She was right to have been worried.

Whatever Principal Greenbeard had said to Mr Brainfright, it had sure taken the wind out of his sails.

'Is everybody ready?' said Mr Brainfright. 'The first word is "jumper".'

'Can you spell that for us?' asked Jack.

'Nice try, Jack,' said Mr Brainfright, 'but I think the idea of a spelling test is that you try to spell the word yourself.'

'Yes, that's correct,' said Fiona.

'Can you put it in a sentence for us?' said David. 'Mrs Chalkboard always did.'

'Of course,' said Mr Brainfright, looking out the window. 'Jumper. It was cold so I put on my jumper.'

We all wrote the word down.

'The next word is "picture",' said Mr Brainfright. 'That is a nice picture on the wall.'

I wondered if he was talking about the picture of the human digestive system or the picture of the inside of a decayed tooth. Neither seemed that *nice* to me.

'Eager,' said Mr Brainfright, stifling a yawn. 'I am eager for this spelling test to end.'

There was laughter. That was more like the Mr Brainfright we'd come to know and love.

'Pyramid,' said Mr Brainfright. 'I was involved in the archaeological dig that uncovered the lost pyramid of King Aha!'

'Is that true?' asked Gretel.

'Oh, yes,' said Mr Brainfright. 'I'll never forget the pyramid of King Aha! It had a curse on it. I didn't believe in curses then. I do now, though.'

'W-what happened?' said Newton.

'I was part of a major international expedition,' Mr Brainfright explained. 'We had been digging for many weeks and then one day I accidentally uncovered the entrance with a single pick swing. The ground underneath me gave way and before I knew it I'd fallen through an intricate system of corridors right into the central chamber of the tomb. King Aha! wasn't too happy, I can tell you!'

'King Aha! was still alive?' said Jack.

'Not exactly,' said Mr Brainfright, 'he'd been dead for over three thousand years . . . but his mummified remains were lively enough! The mummy came at me across the chamber like a freight train. Headbutted me right in the stomach. Knocked me on my back and completely winded me. It was attempting to smother me when I drew my dagger and reduced the mummy to a pile of harmless bandages.'

'And that was the end of it?' asked Jenny.

'The physical end of it, yes,' said Mr Brainfright. 'But the mummy still visits me regularly in my dreams to finish what it started and fulfil the curse. Not that I mind too much. It keeps me on my toes and my dagger skills are second to none. It's a vicious beast, though. If I don't turn up at school one day, you'll know that the mummy has finally got the better of me.'

We all just stared at Mr Brainfright.

Well, all except Newton, who had his eyes shut tight.

The last bell rang.

We all jumped.

Newton screamed.

'Class dismissed,' said Mr Brainfright.

We left the class slowly, our heads full of rampaging mummies.

41
Meeting

'Do you think he was telling the truth?' said Gretel, as we stood at the lockers.

'Probably not,' said Jack. 'But it was a great story. Really freaky.'

'You can say that again,' said Newton. 'I'm not going to be able to sleep tonight. Or tomorrow night. Probably all week.'

'It must be true,' said Jenny. 'He's a teacher. Teachers don't tell lies. Well, they're not supposed to.'

'They're not supposed to fall out classroom windows, either,' said Gretel. 'But *he* does. What do you think, Henry?'

'I think we should ask him to help us find the treasure,' I said.

'Are you kidding?' said Jack. 'He's a teacher. He's on *their* side. He won't let us keep it.'

'In case you hadn't noticed, Mr Brainfright

isn't like the other teachers,' I said. 'Even when he tries to be, he can't do it for long. And don't forget, despite all our effort, we don't even have the treasure. And there's no guarantee we'll ever get it, either. Mr Brainfright has been on an archaeological dig. He discovered a whole tomb! He's our best chance.'

'You're right, Henry,' said Jenny. 'And Skull Island's not going to be ours forever. Sooner or later Fred will realise we've given him a fake map, and then he'll be back.'

'And mad,' said Newton with a shiver. 'Maybe even madder than King Aha!'s mummy!'

'I agree with Henry,' said Gretel. 'All in favour of asking Mr Brainfright to help us find the treasure, raise your hand.'

Everybody raised their hand except Jack.

'Sorry, Jack,' said Gretel. 'You're outvoted.'

Jack shrugged. 'Don't say I didn't warn you,' he said.

42
Ask an expert

Gretel, Jenny, Newton, Jack and I went back into the classroom.

Mr Brainfright was sitting at his desk, staring into space.

'Are you okay, Mr Brainfright?' I said.

'Yes, I'm fine,' said Mr Brainfright. 'I'm just listening.'

'Listening to what?' said Jenny.

'To everything!'

We listened.

'I can't hear anything,' said Jenny.

'Listen more carefully,' said Mr Brainfright.

'I can hear a car,' said Gretel.

'And a bird,' said Newton.

'Wind,' said Jack.

'A dog barking,' I said.

'Very good,' said Mr Brainfright. 'There's always something new. Now, to what do I owe the pleasure of this visit?'

'We need your help,' I said, 'with something very old.'

'Only too happy to help,' said Mr Brainfright. 'What's the problem?'

'Can you keep a secret?' I said.

'Of course,' said Mr Brainfright.

'Cross your heart and hope to die, stick a needle in your eye?'

'Well, I'm happy to cross my heart,' said Mr Brainfright. 'Not so keen on the dying . . . or the needle, for that matter.'

'All right,' I said, 'we'll let you off that. It's about treasure. Buried treasure.'

'Ah,' said Mr Brainfright. 'Very interesting. Where is this buried treasure?'

'That's the trouble,' I said. 'We don't know exactly. But we do know it's buried in the school grounds.'

'Any idea where?' asked Mr Brainfright.

'Somewhere on that hill,' I said, pointing out the window.

'I see,' said Mr Brainfright. 'Well that narrows it down to quite a manageable search. But tell me, how did you find out about this treasure?'

I told Mr Brainfright the whole story. I told him everything that Principal Greenbeard had told me and about our efforts to locate the treasure. I even showed him the key.

156

At the end of my tale, Mr Brainfright's eyes were shining. 'Don't worry,' he said. 'Leave it to me. If there's treasure there, we'll find it . . . or my name isn't Thaddeus Harold Brainfright!'

43
Preparation

The next morning Mr Brainfright was not wearing his purple jacket.

Or his orange shirt.

Or his bright green tie.

He was wearing a khaki shirt and shorts, a pith helmet and a pair of dusty brown boots.

At the front of the classroom was a large pile of spades, picks and shovels. Next to these there were a few bundles of thin wooden stakes and some balls of twine.

'Uh-oh,' said Fiona. 'Looks like Mr Brainfright has got treasure fever too.'

'Good morning, 5C,' said Mr Brainfright. 'I hope you've all had a good breakfast because we have a big morning ahead of us. How many of you have been on an archaeological dig before?'

We all shook our heads.

'Does digging for buried treasure count?' said David.

'It could,' said Mr Brainfright. 'But often what archaeologists are looking for is not what we think of as "treasure", but very ordinary everyday objects that allow us to build up a picture of how people lived in the past. In this sense, a piece of what you might at first think of as junk, such as a piece of chipped pottery, could be regarded as a great treasure.'

'I'd rather find treasure than dumb old bits of chipped pottery,' said Clive.

'The point is, though,' said Mr Brainfright, 'that you never know what you're going to find. That's what makes it so exciting. Now, I know you've all been looking for buried treasure this week so I thought it might be an ideal opportunity to teach you some of the tricks of the trade. What do you think?'

The class nodded enthusiastically.

Not that anybody wanted to find bits of chipped pottery.

We all had one thing on our minds.

Buried treasure.

Proper buried treasure.

The only person not nodding enthusiastically was Jack. 'I knew we shouldn't have told a teacher!' he said. 'Now we'll have to share the treasure with the rest of the class.'

'Well, they were all looking for it anyway,' said Gretel.

'Yeah, but not in the right spot,' said Jack. 'They were never going to find it.'

'Neither were we,' I said. 'Sharing *something* will be better than not having anything to share at all.'

'Henry's right, Jack,' said Jenny. 'Let's not be greedy. Besides, if this treasure is half as valuable as we think it is, there's going to be more than enough to go around.'

Jack shrugged. 'Whatever,' he said.

'Now, we're going to do this systematically,' said Mr Brainfright. He went to the window and pointed at Skull Island. 'We'll begin by pegging out that hill into twenty-five equal squares. You'll have a square each, approximately three paces long on each side. I want each of you to take four wooden stakes, some twine and a pick or a shovel. Let's go!'

44
The big dig

Jenny, Gretel, Jack, Newton and I rushed for the equipment so we could be first to claim the area where we'd already been digging.

I figured that if anybody deserved to find that treasure it was us.

We each measured out our squares and tied twine around the four stakes to mark them clearly.

'What do we do now?' said David from another square.

'Clear the ground,' said Mr Brainfright. 'After you've examined the surface you may start to dig. But do it carefully. The trick is not to destroy what we are looking for.'

'What if we find a mummy?' Newton asked nervously.

'Well, in that case you *should* destroy it,' said Mr Brainfright grimly. 'Destroy it before it destroys you.'

Newton began to tremble. 'I don't want to do this anymore,' he said.

'He's joking, Newton,' I said.

'No, I'm not,' said Mr Brainfright.

'He is, really,' I whispered to Newton.

Newton looked uncertain. He swung his pick half-heartedly.

Everybody else was busy digging. Well, when I say digging, I mean attacking their square of earth with every ounce of energy they had.

It wasn't so much an orderly archaeological dig as complete and utter mayhem.

The air was thick with picks, spades and flying dirt.

'Be careful, now,' called Mr Brainfright above the din. 'Don't forget to be careful!'

But his words were lost in the treasure-digging frenzy.

Clive was smashing his patch of dirt apart with a pick.

Gretel was digging with so much determination and strength that an earthmoving machine would have had trouble keeping up with her.

Fiona was on her hands and knees throwing dirt over her shoulder with a small trowel. The dirt was showering all over David, but he was too intent on digging his own hole to notice, or even care.

Gina and Penny were the only ones not digging. They were too busy trotting around on their imaginary horses, using the twine as jumps.

One thing was for sure, though.

If there *was* buried treasure here, 5C was going to find it.

Whether the treasure would survive the excavation—well, that was another question. But we *would* find it.

I could see students from other classrooms looking enviously out their windows at us.

All the students at Northwest Southeast Central had been spending every minute outside of class time searching for the treasure, but we were the only ones lucky enough to be able to search *during* class time.

This fact was not lost on Mrs Cross, who soon appeared and began marching up the hill towards us.

'What on earth is going on here?' she yelled.

'An archaeological dig!' said Mr Brainfright.

'An archaeological dig?' said Mrs Cross. 'But archaeology is not in the fifth-grade syllabus!'

'It is now,' said Mr Brainfright.

Mrs Cross shook her head. 'You shouldn't be destroying the school grounds like this,' she said. 'It's not right.'

'We're not digging up the school grounds,'

said Mr Brainfright. 'We're conducting an archaeological dig.'

'I don't care what you call it!' said Mrs Cross. 'It's destructive and unnecessary as far as I'm concerned. And I'm not the only one. All the digging of the last few days has upset poor Mr Spade so much that he's had to take stress leave. I should have known you were behind it all.'

'We'll fill it back in again when we've finished,' said Mr Brainfright.

'You're finished now, Brainfright,' said Mrs Cross. 'I'll give you and your class fifteen minutes to fill in your holes, pack up your rubbish, and leave this hill EXACTLY as it was! Otherwise I will be notifying Principal Greenbeard of this deviation from the program . . . and you know what that means!'

Mrs Cross turned and stomped back down the hill.

Mr Brainfright shrugged. He had the same sort of sad look on his face that he'd had after Principal Greenbeard had bawled him out in the corridor the day before.

'I'm afraid we're going to have to finish our dig there, everybody,' he said quietly. 'Could you please begin to fill in your—'

'I've found something, sir!' said Gretel.

Gretel's square was right next to mine. I looked into the hole she'd dug; it was twice as deep as mine. At the bottom I could just make out the shape of a box.

Mr Brainfright came across. 'What have you found, Gretel?' he asked.

'Well,' she said, 'I was digging and my spade made a clunking sound. I think there's something there.'

Mr Brainfright was down on his stomach, scraping dirt away with his hands. 'I think you're right,' he said excitedly. 'But given Mrs Cross's ultimatum, it's going to take us too long to dig it out by hand. I have the exact tool we need in my car. I'll be right back!'

45
Jackhammer

What happened next is going to sound kind of crazy, but I swear it's the truth.

Mr Brainfright returned with a jackhammer.

Now I'm not sure how many people—or teachers—drive around with jackhammers in their cars, but Mr Brainfright was obviously one of them.

And I really wasn't quite sure how the use of a jackhammer fitted with Mr Brainfright's instructions that archaeological digs needed to be conducted with EXTREME care, but I guess we *were* running out of time.

Mrs Cross had given us fifteen minutes, and it would take a lot longer than that to dig the box out carefully.

'Wow, is that a single-phase demolition breaker?' said Grant, clearly impressed.

'Yes,' said Mr Brainfright, as he lowered it down

into the hole. 'It's small, but it gets the job done. Stand back everyone, and block your ears—it's a little bit loud.'

'A little bit loud' was putting it mildly. It was a BIG bit loud. When Mr Brainfright started it up, we didn't only hear it, we *felt* it!

It made the ground tremble.

It made our feet, legs, chests and arms shake.

It made our teeth rattle in our jaws.

And the noise was unbelievable!

I never knew such a small machine could make such a commotion.

Even with my hands pressed hard against my ears the noise hurt.

Mr Brainfright and his single-phase demolition breaker were just a vibrating blur in the middle of a cloud of dust.

And then Mrs Cross appeared.

'That's enough, Brainfright!' she yelled, her shrill tones clearly audible above the noise of the jackhammer.

Even Mr Brainfright heard her.

He shut the jackhammer off.

'Just a couple more minutes and I'll be done,' he pleaded.

But Mrs Cross was firm. 'You're done, all right. You're done RIGHT NOW!'

'But Mrs Cross,' said Mr Brainfright. 'I'm so close!'

'You're more than close,' said Mrs Cross. 'This time you've gone TOO FAR! I'm trying to teach and you're turning the school into a construction zone. You have blown your last chance! I'm going to see that you never teach at this—or any other—school ever again! If "teach" is the right word to describe the bizarre activities you waste your class's time with!'

Mrs Cross marched back down the hill, but not towards her classroom.

She was headed towards Principal Greenbeard's office!

46
Goodbye, Mr Brainfright

Mr Brainfright shook his head sadly and climbed out of the hole.

'I think our work is finished here today,' he said. 'I'm sorry, class. So close and yet so far!'

'Never mind,' said Jenny. 'At least we tried. We gave it our best shot.'

'Yes, we did,' said Mr Brainfright.

The school PA system crackled to life.

'Mr Brainfright is to report to the principal's office immediately,' ordered Mrs Rosethorn. 'Mr Brainfright to the principal's office. IMMEDIATELY!'

Mrs Rosethorn was no more pleasant over the PA than she was in person.

'Grade five,' said Mr Brainfright, 'if I should not return, I want you to know that I've enjoyed my time with you very much. I've learned a lot, and I'm going to miss you all.'

'What are you talking about?' said Gretel. 'You'll be back! You're just going to the principal's office.'

'I think we have to face facts here,' said Mr Brainfright, 'and the fact is that Mrs Cross has got it in for me.'

'Nobody listens to her!' said Jack. 'She's just a cross old busybody!'

'Principal Greenbeard listens to her, Jack,' said Mr Brainfright. 'And I'm rather afraid that he's going to make me walk the plank.'

'Yikes!' said Newton.

'In a manner of speaking,' said Mr Brainfright, patting Newton on the shoulder.

Fiona cleared her throat. 'As co-class captain,' she said, 'on behalf of 5C, I would just like to say that we've really enjoyed having you as our teacher. And I think we've learned a lot, too.'

'Hear, hear!' said David.

Gretel stepped forward and shook Mr Brainfright's hand.

Mr Brainfright's face scrunched up like he was going to cry. 'Gretel,' he said, 'could you let go of my hand? You're crushing it!'

'Sorry, sir,' she said.

'That's quite all right, Gretel,' he said. 'You just have a very strong grip.'

He began walking down the hill.

We were all silent.

None of us knew what to say.

At the bottom of the hill he turned and waved. 'Don't forget how to breathe!' he called. 'And watch out for that window!'

I never cry—well, hardly ever—but I don't mind admitting that I was blinking back tears. Jenny was sobbing. We were watching the best teacher we'd ever had walking away from us.

Don't get me wrong: we liked Mrs Chalkboard all right—but we *loved* Mr Brainfright.

And the worst thing was that it was all my fault he was leaving. If I hadn't encouraged him to start digging for treasure, he wouldn't have organised the archaeological dig, and if he hadn't organised the archaeological dig, Gretel wouldn't have found the treasure chest, and if Gretel hadn't found the treasure chest, then Mr Brainfright wouldn't have gone and got a jackhammer, and if Mr Brainfright hadn't gone and got a jackhammer, then Mrs Cross wouldn't have got quite so cross, and if Mrs Cross hadn't got quite so cross, she wouldn't have gone to Principal Greenbeard, and Principal Greenbeard wouldn't have called Mr Brainfright to his office, and then . . . and then . . . and then I had an idea—a BRILLIANT idea.

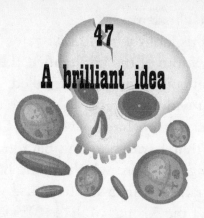

47
A brilliant idea

I jumped into the hole and started digging.

Mr Brainfright's efforts had revealed the top half of a wooden box. It wasn't possible to pull it out just yet, but it wouldn't take very much more digging before it was.

'What are you doing, Henry?' Jenny called out. 'How can you keep digging at a time like this? We're about to lose the best teacher we've ever had and all you care about is some stupid old treasure! Don't you have any feelings at all?'

'No,' I said, 'you don't understand! We have to get the treasure. It's our only hope!'

'Of what?' said Jenny. 'Of getting rich?'

'No,' I said, 'of saving Mr Brainfright.'

'How?' Gretel asked.

'I can't explain now,' I said, still digging hard. 'There's no time. Just help me get the treasure!'

'Out of the way, McThrottle,' said Gretel. 'I

can dig faster than you can!'

I jumped out of the hole and Gretel jumped in.

Armed with a pick, she made short work of it, and moments later she held up a small dirt-encrusted wooden treasure chest with a grinning skull on top of it. I couldn't blame the skull for grinning. I think I'd be grinning too if, finally, after all those years in the dirt, somebody had dug me up. (Although if I'd been buried all those years I'd probably be dead and not grinning at all, so ignore that last comment.)

'Wow,' said Jack, in genuine awe of Gretel. 'You were almost as fast as Mr Brainfright's jackhammer.'

'Almost?' said Gretel. 'I'd like to see the jackhammer that could beat me!'

She handed me the chest. 'So how is this going to save Mr Brainfright?' she asked, still panting with the effort of digging it out.

'Well,' I said, 'the treasure originally belonged to Principal Greenbeard, right? I figure if we can get the treasure to him now, he'll be so happy to have it back, he won't fire Mr Brainfright!'

'Brilliant thinking, Henry!' said Jenny.

'Let's open it first, though, and make sure the treasure is there,' said Jack. 'It might just make Principal Greenbeard angrier if he gets his treasure chest back after all these years and it's empty.'

'Good thinking, Jack,' said Jenny. 'We don't want to make the situation any worse than it already is.'

'No problem,' I said. 'I have the key right here.'

I reached into my pocket and pulled it out.

The grinning skull on the key matched the grinning skull on the chest perfectly.

I was about to push the key into the lock when Newton blew his whistle.

It was almost as loud as Mr Brainfright's jackhammer.

'What are you doing, Newton?' said Jack.

'Danger!' Newton wheezed.

'What danger?' said Jack.

'What if the treasure has a curse on it and mummies start attacking us in our dreams?'

'Don't worry about it, Newton,' said Jack. 'If they try anything just blow your whistle: that will fix them!'

'Mummies can't hear anything,' said Fiona. 'They've got bandages all over their ears, remember?'

'I think Newton's whistle will pierce through a few old bandages,' said Jack.

'It won't happen anyway,' I said. 'You're mixing up pirate treasure with Egyptian treasure. They're two completely different things!'

'Of course,' said Jenny. 'Henry's right. There's no need to be worried about mummies, Newton.'

I pushed the key into the lock.

And turned it.

Well, I *tried* to turn it, but it wouldn't move.

'It's not working!' I said.

'It has to work,' said Jenny.

'Well, it isn't,' I said.

'Don't worry,' said Grant. 'Let me try. I've got a digital skeleton key. Opens anything. It's brand new. My dad invented it last night.'

Jack rolled his eyes.

I shrugged. 'It's worth a try,' I said.

Grant produced a shiny black tube that looked more like a torch than a key. He placed it over the keyhole and pushed a button. It made a series of beeps and clicks. It glowed red. Then it started smoking.

'Grant . . .' said Jack.

'Almost there,' he said.

'Is smoke supposed to be coming out of the end?' Jack asked.

'I don't know,' said Grant. 'I've never used it before.'

'It looks like it's going to explode,' said Jack.

Suddenly Grant's digital skeleton key exploded.

'I hate to say I told you so,' said Jack, 'but I told you so.'

Grant shook his head. 'Maybe the lock's too old,' he said.

'And then again,' said Jack, 'maybe, just maybe, the digital skeleton key doesn't work.'

'Impossible!' said Grant. 'My dad invented it!'

'Exactly!' said Jack.

'That's enough, Jack,' said Gretel. 'This isn't exactly helping us to get the chest open. What we need here is good old-fashioned non-digital brute force. Stand back! This is a job for One-punch!'

Gretel rolled up her sleeve. She clenched her fist, took a deep breath, and then punched the top of the chest.

But, incredibly, despite the power of Gretel's fist, which was strong enough to knock somebody out with just one punch, the chest did not break open.

Gretel's fist just bounced off it. 'Ouch!' she said, shaking her hand. 'That's one tough treasure chest!'

We all stared at it.

The skull's grin seemed to be even wider than before, almost as if it was enjoying our desperate attempts to crack the lock.

Time was running out.

Unless we could open the chest we were going to lose the best teacher we'd ever had!

Then Jenny smiled. 'I've got it!' she said, removing her smiley badge, and getting down on her hands and knees. She began poking around in the lock with the pin of her badge.

'Are you trying to pick the lock?' I said.

'No,' she said, 'I'm cleaning it. The reason the lock won't open is that it's clogged with dirt.' She picked and poked and prodded. 'That's got it! Try the key now, Henry.'

I pushed the key in . . .

and turned . . .

and . . .

the lock clicked.

The chest was open!

But before I could lift the lid, Newton blew his whistle again.

'Newton!' I said. 'Stop blowing that stupid whistle! I already told you, there's no curse!'

But it wasn't the curse Newton was trying to warn me about.

It was worse.

48
Fred's revenge

Two hands reached down from above and picked up the treasure chest.

'I'll take that, thanks very much,' said a familiar voice.

I looked up.

It was Fred.

'That treasure is ours,' I said. 'We found it.'

'And I'm most appreciative,' said Fred. 'But I shouldn't have to remind you that I am the rightful owner of the chest and its contents. We made a deal, remember?'

'That was just for the map,' I said. 'The deal was that I gave you the map and you wouldn't squeeze my neck so that my head popped like a pimple. There was nothing about the treasure in that deal.'

'Yeah, but you double-crossed me,' said Fred, hugging the chest tightly. 'You gave me a fake map, so the deal's off and the treasure is mine.'

'That doesn't make any sense at all,' said Fiona. 'It's neither fair nor reasonable! And what are you doing here, anyway? Shouldn't you be in class?'

'Mrs Cross went to Greenbeard's office,' said Fred. 'And she left me in charge. I gave myself permission to come out here.'

'But that means no one's in charge,' said Fiona. 'If you ask me, that's very irresponsible behaviour.'

'The thing is,' said Fred, stepping up eyeball to eyeball with Fiona, 'nobody is asking you, are they? How about you mind your own business or I squeeze *your* neck until *your* head pops? Does that sound fair and reasonable?'

'Sounds perfectly fair and reasonable to me,' said Fiona, backing away.

'Not to me, it doesn't,' said Gretel. 'Give us the treasure, Durkin . . . or you'll regret it!'

'No,' said Fred coolly, '*You'll* be the one who regrets it. Need I remind you that you already hurt your hand on the chest? I saw you from my classroom. You won't be punching anybody for quite some time.'

'Darn!' said Gretel, rubbing her sore hand.

'Good one, Fred,' said Clive.

'All right, then,' said Fred. 'Now that we've got that all sorted out, let's see exactly what my treasure is.'

Despite our fear and dislike of Fred, the whole class couldn't resist crowding in around him.

Fred took a deep breath and lifted up the lid.

49

What we EXPECTED to see in the treasure chest

1. Gold.
2. Rubies.
3. Emeralds.
4. Diamonds.
5. Bracelets.
6. Coins.
7. Strings of pearls.
8. Rings.
9. Jewel-encrusted daggers and goblets.
10. Pieces of eight (whatever they are).

50
What we ACTUALLY saw in the treasure chest

1. A marble.
2. A rock.
3. A pencil.
4. A yo-yo.
5. A shark's tooth.
6. A rabbit's foot.
7. A black eye-patch.
8. A plastic ring.
9. A water pistol
10. A football card.

51
How to disrespect a Durkin

Fred threw the chest onto the ground. 'This isn't treasure!' he cried. 'It's just a bunch of worthless junk! You're a moron, McThrottle!'

'It's not my fault!' I said. 'I didn't bury it! And I didn't tell you to steal it from me. If anyone's a moron around here it's—'

'Henry,' said Jenny, 'my mother says that if you can't say something nice about a person, then don't say anything at all.'

Jenny's mother was right, of course. But it was too late. The word jumped out before I could shut my lips. 'YOU!' I shouted.

Uh-oh.

'Right, that does it!' said Fred, enraged. 'I'll teach you to disrespect a Durkin!'

He lunged straight at me.

I braced myself.

But he never arrived.

Instead, Newton stuck out his leg and Fred tripped, stumbled, and fell headfirst into the hole where the treasure had been.

The class cheered.

'Nice going, Newton!' I said.

'I'm going to tell my brother you did that!' said Clive.

'I already KNOW he did it, you idiot!' yelled Fred. 'Help me out of here!'

'I didn't mean to do it,' said Newton, looking terrified. 'It was an accident!'

'Accidents happen,' I said. 'Don't worry about it.'

I looked at Greenbeard's treasure lying on the ground.

It might have looked like junk, but given how excited my dad still got about the stuff he'd collected when he was young, I figured there was a pretty good chance that Principal Greenbeard would feel the same way about the things in his treasure chest.

'Come on!' I said to Gretel, Jack, Jenny and Newton. 'Help me pick all this up. We have to get it to Greenbeard's office—fast!'

52
To the rescue

We picked the treasure up off the ground, put it back into the chest and ran as fast as we could to Principal Greenbeard's office.

When we entered the reception area I could hear shouting. It was coming from inside Principal Greenbeard's office.

I hoped we weren't too late.

Mrs Rosethorn was standing at the counter. 'And where do you think you're all going?' she said, giving us all the laser stare. But this time her stare didn't scare me. If we were going to save Mr Brainfright, there was no time to waste being scared.

'I'll explain later!' I said, heading straight for Principal Greenbeard's office.

'Oh, no, you won't!' said Mrs Rosethorn, stepping out from behind her counter and blocking Principal Greenbeard's door with her outstretched arms. 'You'll explain right now!'

'By the time I explain, it may be too late,' I said. 'Please let us in. Please!'

But Mrs Rosethorn shook her head. 'Nobody goes in or out of Principal Greenbeard's office without my permission. Especially not a bunch of dirty scruffy children who don't even have an appointment!'

I took a deep breath. 'So you're not going to let us in?' I said.

'No!' said Mrs Rosethorn firmly. 'And don't waste any more time asking!'

'We're not the time wasters here,' I said. 'You are!'

'How dare you accuse me of wasting time!' Mrs Rosethorn gasped. 'I have never wasted a moment of my time—or anyone else's—in my entire life!'

'Well, I'm sorry, Mrs Rosethorn,' I said, 'but in this case that's exactly what you're doing. Gretel? Would you remove Mrs Rosethorn from the doorway, please?'

'Certainly,' said Gretel, opening her arms wide.

'Don't even think about it, young lady!' warned Mrs Rosethorn.

But Gretel just smiled.

She clamped her powerful arms around Mrs Rosethorn. Then, picking her up as if she were no heavier than a doll, Gretel deposited her back behind the reception desk.

Mrs Rosethorn was too surprised to protest.

'You go in,' said Gretel, standing in the doorway to prevent Mrs Rosethorn from escaping. 'I'll wait here.'

'You kids are in *such* big trouble,' said Mrs Rosethorn.

'We'll see about that,' I said, opening the door.

53
Return of the treasure

We piled into Principal Greenbeard's office.

Mr Brainfright and Mrs Cross were standing in front of Principal Greenbeard's desk with their backs to us.

Mrs Cross was shouting. 'I simply cannot teach as long as he remains at this school! Especially not with all this digging going on. It's disruptive and extremely dangerous! Either he goes . . . or I do!'

Mrs Cross drew a deep breath, and I'm sure she would have kept ranting except that Principal Greenbeard held up his hand. 'Excuse me, Mrs Cross,' he said. He turned his attention to us. 'What is the meaning of barging in here unannounced?'

Mrs Cross and Mr Brainfright wheeled around in surprise.

Jenny, Jack, Newton and I stood to attention and saluted.

'We're really sorry for the interruption, Principal Greenbeard,' I said, 'but we thought you would want to see this.'

I stepped forward and placed the chest on his desk. Then I opened the lid and stood back.

Principal Greenbeard stared at the treasure.

Mrs Cross stared at the treasure.

Mr Brainfright stared at us, beaming.

'My treasure!' said Principal Greenbeard. He was happily pulling things out of the chest and examining them. 'My pirate eye-patch *and* my shark's tooth! I never thought I'd see them again!'

I'd been right about how excited old people get about stuff from their childhoods. So far, so good: my plan was working perfectly.

'But how did you find it?' said Principal Greenbeard, shaking his head.

'It was all Mr Brainfright's idea,' I said quickly. 'I told him about the buried treasure and he's an expert archaeologist so he came up with the idea of conducting a proper archaeological dig to find it.'

'But how did you know where to look?'

'The clue was in the note,' I said. 'I kept thinking about the line "dig for one thousand nights and a night" and then I remembered there is a book called *The Book of the Thousand and One Nights*. So we went to the library and found a copy.'

'Yes,' said Jenny excitedly. 'And we found a story about a man who goes searching for treasure only to find that it was buried right where he started—in his own backyard.'

Principal Greenbeard frowned as he tried to figure out what we were saying. 'So the treasure was . . . ?'

'Exactly where you started,' I said. 'It was on Skull Island all along.'

Principal Greenbeard slapped his forehead. 'Of course,' he said. 'Brilliant!'

Mrs Cross made a strange little sound in her throat.

I looked at her, expecting her to look cross.

But she didn't look cross. She looked scared.

Principal Greenbeard had begun to examine the chest itself.

'What a magnificent treasure chest!' he said, holding it up and looking at it from all sides. 'I would have given anything to have one as good as this. I wonder who it belonged to? The person who stole our treasure, I guess. Hang on, look! The letters W.S. are carved into the bottom.'

He sat there, staring into space and repeating 'W.S.' to himself over and over, as if he was on the verge of remembering something very important.

Mrs Cross was looking more and more upset.

Her face was bright red. There were beads of perspiration running down her forehead.

'Wendy Smith!' Principal Greenbeard suddenly cried.

He fixed his gaze on Mrs Cross, who was already backing away from his desk towards the door. 'It was YOU!' he said. 'You're the scoundrel who stole my treasure!'

Mr Brainfright looked from Principal Greenbeard to Mrs Cross and then back again. 'But how can that be?' he said. 'Her initials are W.C.!'

'She wasn't always Cross!' Principal Greenbeard explained. 'Cross is her married name. Before she was married her name was Wendy Smith and her initials were W.S.!'

54
Mrs Cross escapes

The door slammed.

Mrs Cross was gone.

'I knew it!' said Jack. 'I knew all along there was something fishy about Mrs Cross.'

'Did you?' said Jenny. 'You're so smart, Jack! I never suspected a thing.'

'Funny you never mentioned it,' I said to Jack.

'You never asked,' he said.

'Well don't just stand there like a bunch of leg-locked landlubbers!' said Principal Greenbeard. 'Seize her!'

Newton ran out of the room, blowing his whistle as he went.

'Don't worry, sir,' I said. 'It's under control.'

A few moments later, Gretel came into the office holding Mrs Cross, who was kicking and struggling. Newton followed, still blowing his whistle.

'Well done, Newton,' shouted Jenny, 'but you can stop blowing your whistle now.'

Mrs Rosethorn was hot on Gretel's heels. 'I'm very sorry, sir,' she said to Principal Greenbeard. 'I tried to stop them from disturbing you—'

But nobody was listening to Mrs Rosethorn.

'Let me go,' demanded Mrs Cross, struggling to free herself from Gretel's iron grip.

'Do you promise not to run away again?' said Gretel.

'I promise,' said Mrs Cross.

'Let her go,' said Principal Greenbeard.

Gretel released her.

Mrs Cross sniffed, squared her shoulders and faced Principal Greenbeard.

'Well, Wendy *Smith*,' he said, 'what do you have to say for yourself? Why did you steal our treasure?'

'Because I was angry!' said Mrs Cross. 'You and your friends would never let me play pirates. You were always mean to me. Always chasing me away.'

Principal Greenbeard looked embarrassed. 'Well, er, um,' he said, 'only boys can be pirates. Everybody knows that.'

'That's nonsense,' said Mrs Cross. 'Girls can be pirates, too!'

'She's right, you know,' said Mr Brainfright.

'Female pirates have been around since at least 600 BC! Let me see, there was Lady Mary Killigrew, the daughter of a pirate who became one herself . . . Lai Choi San of Macau, also known as the Dragon Lady . . . Grace O'Malley, the Sea Queen of Connaught . . . and, of course, Sadie the Goat.'

'Sadie the Goat?' said Principal Greenbeard.

'Yes,' said Mr Brainfright, chuckling. 'She used to headbutt her victims before taking their money. Female pirates were every bit as colourful and terrifying as their male counterparts.'

Jenny, Jack, Newton, Gretel and I all looked at one another. We weren't sure whether he was making it up or not.

'I stole your treasure,' Mrs Cross confessed to Principal Greenbeard, 'because I wanted to teach you and the other boys a lesson. I wanted to prove that girls are just as good at being pirates as boys.'

'I think you proved your point,' said Principal Greenbeard.

'Yes,' said Mrs Cross, 'except for the fact that I lost the map I'd drawn. I was going to return the treasure to you, I promise, but I could never find it again. I'm very sorry.'

'Please, Mrs Cross,' said Principal Greenbeard. 'You don't have to apologise. It's not easy for a crusty old sea-dog like myself to admit that I was wrong, but I was. I was totally out of line, and I'm very sorry. If it hadn't been for my ignorance of the glorious history of female piracy, I would have let you join our gang and none of this would ever have happened.'

'No,' said Mrs Cross, 'the fault is all mine. I'm sorry that I stole your treasure in the first place. I've always felt guilty about it. But when the students, and then Mr Brainfright, started digging for it, I was worried about what would happen to me if it was found. I would quite understand if you required me to hand in my notice and seek employment elsewhere.'

'Certainly not!' said Principal Greenbeard. 'I think enough time has passed for us both to forgive and forget. It's all water under the bridge. And I don't think there will be any more digging to disturb you . . . unless, of course, you are aware of any more treasure buried on the island?'

'No,' said Mrs Cross. 'And thank you. Could I just ask one favour?'

'Yes,' said Principal Greenbeard. 'What is it?'

'May I have my treasure chest back?'

'Of course,' said Principal Greenbeard, shutting the lid and putting it into her hands. 'It is indeed a fine treasure chest!'

Mrs Cross nodded. 'Thank you,' she said. 'My

grandfather made it for me. I thought it was lost forever.' Then she turned to Mr Brainfright. 'I think I owe you an apology as well. I see that perhaps there is some method in your madness after all.'

Mr Brainfright smiled graciously. 'More madness than method, I'm afraid,' he said, 'but very pleased to be of service.'

'If you have some time one day,' said Mrs Cross, 'I would very much like to talk to you about female pirates. I'm interested in learning more.'

'It would be a pleasure!' said Mr Brainfright. Then he winked at us, as if to say, *See, I told you she liked me*.

I had to hand it to him. Except when he was falling out windows, he sure knew how to land on his feet. With a little help from us, of course.

Principal Greenbeard turned to Mr Brainfright. 'I, too, am in your debt, Thaddeus,' he said. 'You have a job at Northwest Southeast Central School for as long as you want one. Mrs Chalkboard has let me know that she will not be coming back, so your position as teacher of Class 5C is now permanent, if you would like it.'

'What do you think, kids?' said Mr Brainfright. 'Are you sick of me yet?'

'No way!' I said. 'I think you should stay!'

'Me too,' said Jack.

'Me three,' said Newton.

'Me definitely four,' said Jenny.

'Me five,' said Gretel.

'And me six,' said Mrs Cross.

Mrs Rosethorn remained silent. In her eyes, Mr Brainfright was a time waster . . . but then everybody was.

'So what do you say?' said Principal Greenbeard.

'Of course I'll stay,' said Mr Brainfright, beaming, 'but on one condition.'

'Just name it,' said Principal Greenbeard.

'That 5C now be called 5B,' said Mr Brainfright.

'Done,' Principal Greenbeard agreed, shaking Mr Brainfright's hand. 'Good to have you aboard!'

Then Principal Greenbeard turned to me. 'Henry, I truly appreciate the effort to which you and your friends went to locate the treasure. As a reward, I'd like you each to choose a piece of treasure to keep.'

'Thank you, sir,' I said, 'but you don't have to do that. It's *your* treasure!'

'Which I would never have seen again if it hadn't been for you,' said Principal Greenbeard. 'You've earned it. Go on, choose a piece!'

I looked at the treasure. To tell you the truth, there was nothing I particularly wanted, but as

I looked, my hand was mysteriously drawn to the pencil, and before I even realised what I was doing, I'd picked it up.

'I guess I'll take this pencil if you don't mind,' I said. It was green with black stripes and had a little white eraser on the end in the shape of a skull. To this day I still don't know why I picked it up, and I sure came to regret it, but that's a whole other story.

Principal Greenbeard was delighted with my choice. 'I don't mind at all!' he said. 'That pencil belonged to my best friend, Mark Fortuna. He loved that pencil. He's not alive anymore, but I know he'd be happy for you to have it. He was a great one for writing and storytelling—not unlike yourself, Henry.'

'Thanks!' I said. 'I'll take good care of it.' As it turned out, this was a lie because I spent a lot of time trying to destroy it. But, like I said, that's a whole other story.

Then Newton bravely stepped forward. 'May I have the lucky rabbit's foot?' he said. 'I've always wanted a lucky rabbit's foot.'

'Of course!' said Principal Greenbeard, putting it into Newton's hand. 'A bit of extra luck never hurt anyone!'

As Newton's hand closed around the lucky charm he seemed to grow six inches before our eyes. 'Thank you, Principal Greenbeard,' he said, not looking quite as nervous as before.

After that, Gretel chose the shark's tooth, Jack chose the water pistol and Jenny took the ring. After we thanked Principal Greenbeard, he stood to attention and saluted us all.

He picked up the black eye-patch and slipped it on, positioning it over his left eye. 'Thank you, everybody,' he said. 'You've made an old sea-dog very happy.'

55
Learning to fly

We headed back to Skull Island where the rest of the class were trying—not that hard—to get Fred out of the hole. We told them the good news about Mr Brainfright becoming our regular teacher and everybody cheered. Well, everybody except Fred, whose head was still down the hole. Then Gretel lifted Fred out, and we spent the rest of the morning filling in all the holes we'd dug.

When we were settled back at our desks, Mr Brainfright clapped his hands.

We all craned forward, wondering what crazy and amazing lesson he would attempt to teach us this time.

'I'd like you all to take out your *Maths is Fun* textbook and turn to page forty-five,' he said.

Nobody moved. It wasn't exactly what we were expecting.

'Is there a problem?' said Mr Brainfright.

'Yes,' said Fiona.

'But I thought you liked maths, Fiona,' said Mr Brainfright.

'I do,' said Fiona, 'but, well, after learning how to breathe, skid on a banana peel, re-enact history and dig for treasure, maths somehow just doesn't seem as much fun as it used to.'

'Is that so?' said Mr Brainfright, slamming his book shut and frisbeeing it expertly out the window. 'In that case it's lucky I was just kidding! What we're actually going to do today is learn how to fly.'

'With our own personal jet-packs?' asked Grant.

'No,' said Mr Brainfright. 'Like birds. It will come in handy if you are ever jumping out of a plane and your parachute fails! Now, everybody stand up and flap your arms!'

'I'm scared of flying!' said Newton. 'It's dangerous!'

'Not if you have a lucky rabbit's foot, it's not,' said Mr Brainfright. 'And especially not if you keep flapping your arms. It's only when you stop flapping your arms that flying is dangerous.'

I smiled at Jenny. She smiled back.

'Will we be tested on this?' asked Fiona.

56
Mr Brainfright's last really important lesson

It is only when you stop flapping your arms that flying is dangerous.

57
The last chapter

Well, that's my story.

And, just in case you're wondering, it's all true.

Every last bit.

If you're ever passing through Northwest, and you happen to be passing Northwest Southeast Central School, feel free to drop in.

We're pretty easy to find. Our classroom is the first on the left as you go up the steps.

And our teacher wears a purple jacket.

But don't forget to call in at the office first and sign the visitors' book.

And don't waste time while you're doing it. As I think I have mentioned, Mrs Rosethorn does not like time wasters.

Anyway, it would be great to see you, and if you enjoyed that story then don't worry, I've got plenty more!

And they're all true.

Every last one.

Oh, and in case you're wondering, Mr Brainfright *did* teach us to fly. It's not easy, though. You *do* have to keep flapping your arms the whole time.

Schooling Around #2: Pencil of Doom!
Andy Griffiths

The *Pencil of Doom!* Test

1. Henry's scary new pencil has an eraser in the shape of a
A: smiley face. B: love heart. C: skull.

2. The pencil is called a 'pencil of doom' because
A: it used to belong to a boy called Doom. B: it has a very sharp tip. C: whenever it's used, somebody gets hurt.

3. Henry tries to destroy the pencil by
A: eating it. B: kissing it. C: crushing it.

4. Henry's enemy, Clive Durkin, uses the pencil to draw Henry and his friends being buried under an avalanche of
A: rose petals. B: puppies. C: snow.

5. *Pencil of Doom!* is the name of
A: a horror movie. B: a computer game. C: a very funny book about a very dangerous pencil.

ANSWERS
The answers to these questions—and many more—are contained between the covers of this very funny book about a very dangerous pencil.

Schooling Around #3: Mascot Madness!
Andy Griffiths

The *Mascot Madness!* Test

1. Northwest Southeast Central School have never won the interschool athletics competition because they have
A: no talent. B: no guts. C: no mascot.

2. Mr Brainfright dances around in a banana suit because
A: he's bored. B: he's nuts. C: he's the new Northwest Southeast Central mascot.

3. Northwest West Academy's mascot, a ferocious pit bull terrier called Chomp, is trained to attack
A: postmen. B: cats. C: bananas.

4. Mr Grunt, the sports teacher, brags that he was once in the
A: newspaper. B: army. C: Olympics.

5. *Mascot Madness!* is
A: a new dance. B: when a mascot gets angry. C: a very funny book about winning, losing, cheating, really hard squeezing and dancing bananas.

ANSWERS
The answers to these questions—and many more—are contained between the covers of this very funny book about winning, losing, cheating, really hard squeezing and dancing bananas.

Schooling Around #4: Robot Riot!
Andy Griffiths

The *Robot Riot!* Test

1. Henry McThrottle suspects that the new girl, Roberta Flywheel, is
A: a spy. B: a boy. C: a robot.

2. Roberta writes in her diary that she is on a mission to
A: kiss Henry. B: clean up the school. C: exterminate all humans.

3. Henry and his friends get Grant Gadget to build
A: a treehouse. B: a sandcastle. C: a robot-fighting robot.

4. Grant Gadget's robot-fighting robot malfunctions and
A: picks flowers. B: starts telling jokes. C: goes completely out of control.

5. *Robot Riot!* is the name of
A: a soft drink. B: a hairstyle. C: a very funny book about robots, making friends and falling out of windows.

ANSWERS The answers to these questions—and many more—are contained between the covers of this very funny book about robots, making friends and falling out of windows.

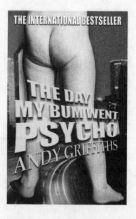

ZOMBIE BUMS FROM URANUS
Andy Griffiths

Zack Freeman is back . . . and so is his bum.

Aided by little more than a squeezy bottle of tomato sauce, a rudimentary grasp of the hokey pokey and three of the oldest bum-fighters on the planet, Zack and his bum are fighting to protect the Earth against an invasion of some of the smelliest and most dangerous bums ever to pollute the universe: zombie bums from Uranus!

Can they prevent the unthinkable—total zombie-bummification of the world?

Be bold, be brave, be entertained beyond your wildest dreams in the heart-stopping, nostril-blasting, zombie-bums-from-Uranus-filled sequel to *The Day My Bum Went Psycho*.

BUMAGEDDON: THE FINAL PONGFLICT
Andy Griffiths

It began with *The Day My Bum Went Psycho*.
It continued with *Zombie Bums from Uranus*.
And now it ends with *Bumageddon: The Final Pongflict*.

Zack, Eleanor and Zack's bum travel back 65 million years in time to put an end to the Great White Bum once and for all. But before they can deal with him, they have to fight some of the biggest, meanest and smelliest bumosaurs ever to stain the face of the Earth, including a pair of angry Tyrannosore-arses, a deadly Tricerabutt, a hungry Bumadactyl and the very stupid—and very smelly—Stink Kong.

'Andy Griffiths' sense of the stupid and subversive goes up to the top of the hill and down the other side in *Bumageddon: The Final Pongflict* . . . the final episode of the adventures of Zack Freeman and his amazing bottom.'
SOUTH CHINA MORNING POST (YOUNG POST)

'If your children like Roald Dahl, they'll enjoy this.'
AUSTRALIAN WOMEN'S WEEKLY